A Crack
Everything

A Crack in Everything

Short Stories

Tales of hope and despair, regret and redemption

JOHN P. ASLING

The Choir Press

First published in the United Kingdom in 2017 by The Choir Press.

ISBN 978-1-911589-31-0

For Claire and Martin
&
Patricia

'There is a crack in everything.
That's how the light gets in.'

LEONARD COHEN

Contents

The Memory Girl

Eve is tired, confused. What has just happened? she wonders. She picks up the faded playing cards, shuffles absently, trying to remember the rules.

*

I spread the playing cards face down on the living room floor and invite Granddad Jacob or Granddad William to sit on a big fat cushion and flip the cards over two at a time to make a match. I love the exotic scent of Granddad Jacob's cigarettes, the sweetness of Granddad William's aftershave. They smile down at me.

'Play with me. Please, Granddad.'

I never forget a card. When the matching card is exposed, I pounce. At the end of the game, I have the most pairs.

'I won again. I must have a much better memory than you.'

I giggle and dance around the living room.

I never forget what is written on the chalkboard. When we move to a comfortable borough the teachers wonder if I get too much help. Mum and Dad sit uncomfortably close on plastic chairs in the head's office, eyes lowered, as the teacher wearing a scoop-necked red jumper struggles to find the right words. Dad smiles gravely.

Mum says, 'I think you will see that Eve has a rather good memory and it shows in her work.'

The teacher nods. In the coming weeks, tests come back near perfect. I am at the head of the class and have many friends, long-legged youngsters, like me.

'Come on, you guys, you have to remember this. You know it's easy.'

My arm high over my head, I lead the charge to the shade of our favourite tree.

'Let's learn this and then we can play again. In fourteen hundred and ninety-two, Columbus …'

*

Eve ambles to the ringing telephone, brushing aside her shock of grey hair as she picks it up. It is her daughter Louise. The doctor is not sure, Eve tells her. They need more tests, more intelligence, she jokes, not laughing. She doesn't mention the incident at the supermarket, losing her car, someone calling the police. She hangs up, thinks of calling her mother but remembers the cancer. When was that?

*

Dad comes home late from the city. I listen to them, playing it back while clutching my pink pillow before falling off to dreamless sleep.

'I've told you it's only work. Just work, nothing more!' he screams across the living room. The front door slams. Mum sobs in the kitchen. A dish crashes, bits scattering across the new linoleum.

Dad moves out. I won't talk to him, freezing family perfection in my head.

The granddads visit less. Granddad Jacob is in Israel and Granddad William is unwell. I pull them into the newly panelled den.

'Okay, Granddad, time to play checkmate.'

We laugh, though they see my puffy eyes. Granddad Jacob's moves are well orchestrated. Granddad William is instinctive. But his game is fading. I know where the pieces on the board are headed. Three moves. Checkmate! I beat them and the joy returns as I brush back my long black hair.

'You'll do better next time, Granddad. I won't be so lucky,' I tell Granddad Jacob.

With Granddad William, I am gentler. 'You must have been sleepy today.'

*

Eve fingers through the black spiral phone book. She doesn't recognize the handwriting. She is looking for Lauren's number. What is her last name?

*

I'm excited about university. Lauren and I want to be lawyers, like the ones we see carrying bulging files to the courthouse.

'We'll take on the City,' I tell her over milky coffees in our Greenwich café.

Studies go well but I lose interest. There's something else I want to do. I don't want to let Lauren down. We were to be colleagues in arms, bringing feminist values to law. Mum and Dad help pay my fees. I don't want to hurt any of them. One night I open up to Lauren.

Lauren sees it coming. 'Eve, with your brain, you can do anything. What do you want to do?'

I pull a wrinkled flyer out of my tiny handbag: *Capture the moment: hold it for a lifetime.* It's for a photography course. 'I just want to try this,' I say.

'Why?' Lauren asks.

'To understand what's going on in the world, explain it, remember better.'

'No one remembers better than you.'

We laugh.

*

Eve fingers through the black spiral phone book. She doesn't recognize the handwriting. She is looking for Lauren's number. What is her last name?

*

I meet Alex on the first day of photography studies. He's tall and gangly, has curly brown hair hanging down his shoulders. We are paired for the first assignments. Alex is an old hand with the technology. I'm a quick learner with a flair for framing the right picture. We wander London's back streets taking stark black-and-white photographs of rough Hackney and Brick Lane, colour shots of architectural oddities in Kensington. We become lovers. I land a job with a wire service in Northern Ireland, Alex with a magazine in Southeast Asia. We have sweet moments together in our Greenwich flat, collapsing on the narrow bed, making love before falling asleep, waking again for pizza and red wine.

Granddad William is slipping. He remains physically strong though doctors say he suffers from a dementia that is getting rapidly worse. I bring my camera and some photographs. I take a photograph of him sitting glumly in his simple room in the care home. He smiles faintly as the flash washes his tired face.

He speaks slowly. 'They say I am losing my memory. No games for me now, love ... I can still remember some things, just not all the time. It's a bit scary ... I can't remember where I put things, where I was going, what I was ... saying. I don't want to lose my memory. There are treasures ...'

I bite my lip.

'And some things worth forgetting,' I whisper.

I hug him goodbye.

The image stays with me: Granddad William sitting idly in his bleak bedroom without a sense of history. 'No games for me now, love.' To lose your memory is a hardship, though there are days ...

We have trouble getting time off together. Alex is distracted. I worry about Granddad William and grab a flight to visit him, arriving late in Greenwich to crash before heading to the home. The lights are on. Alex has delayed his trip to Vietnam. He is there, lying peacefully on the bare stomach of the child-like blonde who pulls pints at the neighbourhood pub. I run out of the flat and into a taxi. Mum greets me wordlessly, our tears mingling.

*

Someone's at the door. A man in a red truck brings a package, a heavy box, stamped with stars and stripes. Eve is not sure whether to open it . . .

*

I work feverishly, trying to capture the Troubles. My work wins an award and I'm invited to mount a small exhibition in London. Mum and Dad attend, sitting on opposite sides of Lauren and her poet with mahogany skin. Dad is with another young woman with red lips, Mum alone. They exchange weary glances.

I speak briefly to the small crowd. 'We don't take every word our religious leaders say as gospel, and we no longer treat our holy books as infallible, yet we regard certain patches of land as sacred enough that we kill to keep them. I hope these photographs give us pause.'

I visit Granddad William. He splutters and spits in hideous laughter. I laugh along, wipe my eyes. I give Granddad William a photograph of a small girl at a Belfast memorial service, the girl's eyes somehow wide with hope.

Granddad William sits quietly looking at the photograph. He whispers, 'I remember you. You're the one with the photos in your head.'

*

Eve turns the pages of a fat scrapbook, placing her long finger on a photograph of a veiled woman surrounded by broken bricks. She wonders who the woman is.

*

I move to the Middle East. A stooped Granddad Jacob meets me. He is a widower, his grey beard scruffy. We hug, oblivious to the strangers in the crowded bus station. We sip tea and share finger food.

'Before you begin your work here, you must spend one afternoon with me,' Granddad Jacob says.

We hold hands as we wander through the Holocaust Museum, atrocity after atrocity portrayed in understated starkness. We walk in a trance past a mosaic of men, women and children, herded like cattle, guns pointed at emaciated bodies. Heads bowed, we listen to the litany of lost children, birthed for slaughter, now just candles in a hall of horrors.

Granddad Jacob breaks the silence. 'You must not forget.'

The Jerusalem bureau is hard work: bureaucratic nightmares, guns and blood. I tramp through overcrowded Palestinian villages and jittery settlements, snapping a child in the rubble, an old man quietly weeping over the death of his family, a woman wailing amid the rubble that was her home.

I go to see Granddad Jacob in the state home in Tel Aviv. He is frail but his mind is alert. I arrive at dusk and find him sipping a cold drink in a common room surrounded by wrinkled women competing for his attention. I wheel his chair to a corner.

'I need to talk to you,' Granddad Jacob begins. 'They say I could die soon.'

'Please, Granddad.'

'Listen, my little world-famous photographer.'

'God,' I gasp.

We laugh.

'I've been thinking about what I said to you a few years ago.' He wipes tonic water from his lips. 'Perhaps I was wrong. Maybe it is better after all to forget. I no longer want to remember ... the look on my mother's face as they took her away. The hunger. The brutality.'

I look down at his scrawny ankles.

'Granddad, you have to remember. It's who you are.'

'I don't know.'

'I want to talk to you too.'

'What is it?'

'About the Palestinians.'

'No.'

'I've learned something of their story. It doesn't mean we have to forget.'

'No, Eve.'

He rarely uses my name. We are quiet. Can there be a balance between remembering your story and holding a place for the experience of others? I think also of Alex, Mum and Dad.

'Granddad, I'm sorry if I upset you.'

'That's enough,' he says.

*

Eve is suddenly scared. What was it the doctor said? She lies down in the tiny guest bedroom in her Greenwich flat. Her own bed is covered in books and newspaper clippings. She leaves her clothes on but takes off her shoes and socks. She is tired but cannot sleep. She stares at the ceiling, cries for no reason, finally falls asleep. She dreams of orchids.

*

I fly to Africa and Latin America for magazines and development agencies, trying to capture the dignity of women struggling to overcome violence at the hands of their husbands, and the dark alleys they inhabit. I meet a diplomat. He sends bouquets of orchids, jewels. We vacation in the Caribbean. I take an apartment in New York. He says he will leave his wife.

I sit in Lauren's refurbished Greenwich flat, drinking weak tea.

'It was a great love, but I wasn't going to put up with years of grief. I can picture how it would have been.'

I hire an assistant and focus on life with my brown-eyed baby. She is etched in my heart. Louise grows like wild grass: a four-year-old drawing pictures; a fourteen-year-old covered with mud on a rugby pitch; an art graduate in New York spattered with clay.

*

When Eve wakes, Louise is there, a jangle of ideas, affections and concern. She begins a mental litany of the growing number of lapses, holds her mother close. Together they open the box Louise has sent ahead from the school in America. It is a sculpture, a present for Eve, made by Louise. It is a woman in smooth black stone, stretching her neck backwards as if to remember, yet looking forward, fearless.

'I call it Memories,*' says Louise.*

A Crack in Everything

I

This is no way to say goodbye but it's the best I can do. The doctor has just left my bedside in this tiny apartment, touching my hand with his cold bony fingers and smiling the grey smirk of a mortician. The cancer that only two years ago left me dry and sexless at sixty years of age and sent you packing for the Indian ashram and your holy man, has returned, and the doctor has declared that I will not make it past nine months.

This was supposed to be my great Canadian novel after all those years of tirelessly selling my soul to make the nuclear power industry look cheerful and healthy. It's true I made more than a few decent pieces of silver and gained a chance to travel the globe tasting its many shades of reds and whites, wine and women, as I went. But now I live with the regret, and instead of a great tome sketching the decline of modern civilization, you get this, an apologist's memoir, part epicurean frolic and part Via Dolorosa. It might be somehow amusing to you if it weren't so bloody real.

God laughs at our plans. A year ago, having apparently beaten the cancer at the expense of the juice of sex, I left my beloved Geneva to return to the Toronto of my youth, finding a furnished apartment three minutes from the lake. (You know well most of my resources went to alimony and drink.) It's not as cheap as I wanted but by cobbling together some of my pension funds and by begging loans and gifts from a few friends, I was able to get this place. (Thank you for sending your rupees along with the Leonard Cohen CDs and books you took when you ran away to Goa.)

The squat old brown box no one has had the heart to tear down is next door to the library where I first read Harper Lee and Vladimir Nabokov, and on the streetcar line that took me downtown to the sweet joints of my youth. It is minutes from where I grew up and where Mom and Dad are buried in the church cemetery where we played hide and seek as children, separated by an impenetrable wall, just as they were in life.

Am I afraid to die? I don't know. What is it they say? It's not the fall that will kill you; it's the landing. But I don't know what will be worse, feeling this wretched body further deteriorate around these brittle old bones or meeting my God and having to make defences for a life lived so imperfectly. That's if I believe in God on that day. There are days of belief and days of wonder now, as there have always been. Who is this God, anyways, but a reflection of what we want out of life: peace one moment, joy the next, the pleasure of touch, the bliss of separation. Such heresy, I know. I remember you laughing as I thrust my semen into you, grabbing your bottom like a ripe fruit and shouting, 'God, fuck me!'

And then you responded precisely, 'So that's who you want.'

I guess we always want God, or another moment of bliss, another love, another chance at life. But now I'm not sure who it is I will meet – or whether it matters. But no God will condemn me more than some of the people I have encountered along the way, particularly those like you who had the misfortune to get too close to me and taste a moment of the intimacy I could fake so well. And no God will judge me more harshly than I have judged myself.

You never got to visit me here (you are such a Euro-snob), but in my medicated dreams we have wandered the old neighbourhood together. I have lain beside you in the soft green ravines of my teens. I have tasted your breast where my hungry mouth first clung to the holy fruit of Tessa, before, in her matter-of-fact manner, she edged me away from her tender nipple, whispering a lesson from those rigid Irish nuns.

'Jack, I can't. That's only for sluts.'

I held you in the back of the ornate confines of my first Confession, the dark pews hugging us just as they embraced Tessa and me in the grips of that death-obsessed Good Friday, as most of our fellow parishioners trudged home to their solemn meal of fish sticks.

I took you to the site of the accident that spilled my youthful blood on to our peaceful street in the shadow of the clock tower and left me nearly blind in my left eye and gave the family a litany of stories that last to this day, though most of them are sadly long buried, lost to alcohol, tobacco, suicide and a stupid bus accident in a Brazilian resort.

I have stood staring across the tennis nets of my youth, pounding the yellow Wilson ball towards you, watching you gleefully picking the corners of the back of the court as Molly once did (practical Molly, my friend, who became my wife, then my friend once again – I think). I have held your hand as we crossed the few cold yards between the graves of my mom and dad, telling you how they met a spitting distance from where they now lie, how the freshness of love grew to a brittle end after forty years of battling, giving up, throwing out.

I don't think I have ever told you that my earliest memory was standing on our east-end Toronto veranda with a mouthful of rusty blood and half my lip hanging down my face, cut on God knows what. The door handle? The jagged bricks of the front wall? We never knew. And the pain, the piercing pain. It was then I first consciously tasted the flesh of a woman as my broad mother scooped me into her arms and pressed me to her breast, blood and human flesh coming together as sacrament.

It was my first remembered pain, my first conscious touch

of female comfort, my First Station, if you will. I was at that moment somehow awakened, and condemned.

II

I've been dreaming again. Anna, my nurse, a dark Filipino beauty, her eyes flooded with mystery, had fixed my pillows just right and given me my sweet medication just a little bit early. She sneaked me a shot of gin as well, though I'm sure the doctor has warned her not to. It's not good to mix your drinks, they say. Hell, at this stage I will do anything to sleep – even dream colourlessly of things I have worked so hard to forget.

> *. . . I am easing out from between two parked cars on Herbert Avenue in our Beach neighbourhood. My right hand is armed with one hard red chestnut whose rich earthy scent I can still smell. My arm is cocked and I'm ready to unload. My left hand grips my reserve ammunition. It is a cool late August afternoon but I am sweating. I am five years old and trembling. It's not like me to be involved in this little war. There are new kids living across the road, Indians, though I don't know if they are native Canadians or from India. They are dark, coloured we call them. We are trying to deliver a message, though I am not sure exactly what it is. I ease out a little further into the road; bring my arm back, aim and fire. Everything goes black . . .*

Why am I taking up that cross again? I am not sure. It's probably just the drugs, or the gin, or the combination. I don't really remember what happened next but I have pieced it together over the years, or filled in the gaps with my imagination, mostly because it is part of the family narrative, our little bit of east-end Toronto folklore. At least it helped my brothers and sisters explain what they called my 'anti-social behaviour' to those who asked about it.

'Jack's like that because of the accident.'

I'm sure you've heard that once or twice before. The local grocery store's delivery truck ran over me. The poor driver never had a chance to stop; he couldn't have seen me until the last second. My baby brother ran up the street to tell my mom, and she came running out of our house, probably wiping her hands on her apron, hoping my brother had somehow got the story wrong. My dad was away on a retreat north of the city with the men of the local parish. It was some kind of Augustinian enclave, where a famous Canadian theologian used to contemplate the state of Roman Catholicism before going through his own private reformation, leaving the priesthood, getting married and then trying to fix the church from the periphery. My dad left them praying for my recovery. Somehow it worked; at least that's the version Dad often slurred into his whiskey. Another version was that the captain of the local fire station gently massaged my head and quickly got me off to the hospital. Only God knows the truth; perhaps it was some combination of the two. I suffered a fractured skull and was in a coma for eighteen hours, but somehow recovered. Most days of my life I've been thankful about that. Sometimes in the past few weeks I've had my doubts.

Anna is becoming much more than a nurse to me. If she reads that sentence she will probably erase it. Sometimes when I haven't even the strength to hold my little computer on my lap, she types my words for me, questioning me in her indirect manner over a word or phrase she doesn't hear or understand. Soon she may have to do all the typing. Anna has moved into the bedroom while I am perched on the extra wide settee in the living room. She shops for us, takes out the rubbish, cooks the little bit I can get down, changes my bedding and does the washing-up. Sometimes in my sleep I think I can feel her tiny dark hands on my bony body, sometimes even reaching down to my groin; sometimes I even imagine I am growing to meet her touch. But I wake up to the reality of my limp libido and hear her gentle snoring in the bed in the next room, the bed I had hoped you would join me in for one last chapter of our love. God, how we were once so hungry for each other, skin hungry, you called it; we were unafraid of tasting each other's nooks and crannies. Or books. You introduced me to Nadine Gordimer, to Chinua Achebe. And music. God, I found your operatic fixation entrancing and loved the way you dressed for *Aida* our posh night out in London, that black dress exposing the freckles on your gorgeous breasts, your long legs slipping in and out of the slit in the floor-length gown. But now you flit back and forth between Geneva and Goa, chasing your lower-case gods and goddesses while I am ripped apart with this demon disease. Why won't you visit me? Why won't you answer my messages? I need you one more time.

... I am thirteen years old, skinny, scared, but with a vague hope for a future of bliss. I am entering St. Francis Minor Seminary run by the Franciscans on a hundred acres of rocky farmland an hour's drive north of Toronto. Father Conor, the tiny Irish-born assistant priest at Corpus Christi Church across from the racetrack in our neighbourhood, thinks I will make a good priest. I am a conscientious altar boy, who loves to be close to the secrets of the holy Latin Mass and the silver monstrance where Jesus is on display in the host Sunday afternoons during Benediction. Still, I am not sure why I am here, though I am not unhappy to be leaving my home. I am sitting on my suitcase while my plump teary-eyed mom talks to a brown friar, who rests a reassuring hand on hers. It is going to cost a lot to send me here, and Mom is now going

back to work after years of raising the five of us. The shiny brown suit I am wearing cost a fortune. I stand up and realize I have ripped the trousers . . .

I am trying to forget my dreams, trying to forget. Anna is busy mixing something in the kitchen. She has helped me by typing my meandering thoughts and dreams, whispered through gin and medicinal tonics. She won't look me in the eye. I feel like a man who lost his leg in the war but still feels the pain where it was. I must keep my pseudo lust for Anna to myself. She is so lovely, though, petite and dark; she moves quickly from kitchen to living room, taking my temperature, washing my face with those sterilized facecloths. Her body looks soft and round beneath that loose grey frock. Why won't she look at me?

. . . Dad is pissed. He comes walking up our street all funny smiles, his tie half off, wearing his jacket around his shoulders, making it look like one of the swashbuckling capes Prime Minister Pierre Elliott Trudeau made famous years later.

'Where is the car?' Mom is furious; crying, but furious.

Dad nonchalantly opens a beer and puts on the television. 'We'll get a new one,' he laughs in her face.

'Which slut were you with this time?' she is screaming, crying, but screaming . . .

I don't want to dream but I keep slipping away. It is the price of feeling no pain. Feeling no pain? Isn't that what we used to say in the 1960s? Is that what I have been searching for all these years?

I am wakened by the sound of a streetcar clicking along my street, my new street, my final street. There have been so many streetcars over the years. I'm not sure what time it is but it might be bringing kids home from the high school, factory workers finishing an early shift, or old fellows like myself out killing time before supper. We used to take the Queen Street streetcar to go to hockey games downtown, watch the Maple Leafs take on the Montreal Canadiens; later on there were bars and those seedy massage parlours. Such were the temptations. And I used to work downtown at Simpson's, the big department store.

... Tessa and I have just gotten off work on a Friday night. It is a twenty-minute ride to our east-end homes from the stores. She makes doughnuts at Eaton's. I wrap parcels at Simpsons, right across Queen Street. She is wearing the short kilt from her Roman Catholic high school and has it hiked up higher than usual. She places my sweaty hand on her soft white thigh. She sets her sweater over my lap and undoes my fly, finds my hard cock. The old red streetcar clicks too quickly along the line. We are oblivious to the world.

Mom is five rows back ...

Now every little pain or bit of breathlessness feels like it is the end. When I mention this, Anna just shakes her head at me, makes like she is praying in her native tongue, though she may be cursing me, or denigrating herself for taking the job. But it has perhaps always been this way. Every bit of pain, perceived pain, must have a fix. Every bad memory must become a gentle dream, day or night. Why is that?

Molly has visited today. Plump Molly. Practical Molly. Molly, my friend. Sitting right beside me and yet somehow a million miles away; distant and supportive at the same time. Just like when we were married.

Anna finds things to shop for down on Queen Street, probably stops at the coffee shop where her friend works, maybe even tells tales from the apartment where the dying man looks at her with such strange desire.

Molly makes tea, but it's too milky and I can't even look at it without feeling nauseous again. I think she wants to talk, maybe even wants to touch me. But she does neither. I stare out the window. The tops of the trees are waving back and forth though I can't even remember what time of year it is. It doesn't matter. It could be any season, any year. Molly is saying something, something kind. I can't hear the words but I recognize the tone of voice. Is she forgiving me? Does she want my forgiveness? I am not sure. I have never been sure with Molly. But she is here. That's all that matters. I try to reach for her hand.

III

Anna is cooking in the tiny kitchen. It smells wonderfully exotic, brings tears to my eyes. I think I recognize some of the spices but the words won't come to me. Am I losing my mind too? It must be the drugs. Then she is changing the sheets, fixing the bed so that I can sit up and type these words. I look away as she cleans up my mess. Anna has been even quieter than usual since Molly visited. I don't even want to ask why. She wouldn't answer anyways. The food no longer smells wonderful. I reach for the plastic bowl on my lap. I can't eat. I am shrivelling away to nothing. All those years of trying to lose weight and now it melts away like a spring snowfall.

Anna is talking about inviting her Filipino priest over for lunch. He's very young, she says, but smart, tells funny jokes before every sermon, loosens people up. I don't know why she wants him to visit. Maybe it is for herself. It can't be easy working here. I didn't really try to kill myself, I tell her again. She just looks away, crosses herself and speaks in her language.

I got up today when she was sleeping - I never get up, rarely anyways - and staggered over to the little locker where she keeps the meds. I just wanted to see how much was left. They told me I would be pain free by now. She won't increase the dosage until the doctor comes. The bastard is on holidays, sunning himself on a Cancun beach. He's bloody older than I am. I just wanted to see how much medication was left. I tried to jig the door open. It wouldn't budge and somehow I knocked the locker over, spilling everything on top, syringes, bandages, ointment and scissors. The locker never opened. I fell down and lay on the cold floor for a long time before Anna helped me up. I might have been crying; I'm not sure. I might have said something stupid about getting this bloody dying over and done with; I'm not sure. But I wasn't trying to kill myself. I am sure of that. Absolutely certain.

Today was a better day. The doctor has come (bastard!) and increased the meds. Anna took the morning off and Molly was here keeping an eye on things (me?). I wonder if Anna called her. She must have. There has been no visit from the young priest. I am feeling okay. Somehow I can cope, as long as I don't look at the doctor's sombre face or Molly's teary eyes. Something has upset her. But I am feeling better. I might even look at the newspaper and see how the Maple Leafs are doing in the standings. When I mention this, Molly almost laughs. I guess it is summer. But she never was one for the hockey. Give her a good book instead. I want to thank her for helping out but nothing comes out of my mouth when I try to speak. I think I will sleep now.

... I am lying in your sweet bed. Molly waits at home. Your body is silk against my pudgy belly and sleeping manhood. I have tasted every inch of you. I am sated. How could sin be so good? How could this be wrong? I am talking too much.

'If only we could spend our lives like this! How I love your body, darling.'

You slowly roll over and get out of the bed, sit down fully naked on the hotel room chair, tall, graceful, statuesque.

'My body, Jack? How do you separate that from the rest of me?'

I struggle for words . . .

Anna's priest is here. I refuse to talk to him. He is a small man, almost pretty, dressed impeccably in black. He offers me one of those tasteless wafers I used to adore. I turn away. Then he presses a small wooden crucifix into my shrivelled hand. I make a fist and the cross cuts my palm.

. . . I am seven years old, shivering in the early-morning stench of my nightly piss. I hear Dad clomping up the stairs. No, please, not again. He pulls his thick leather belt from his trousers . . .

IV

Anna bundles me into the wheelchair she brought from the hospital where she used to work and is pushing me up Kingston Road towards the cemetery. Somehow I got it into my mind this morning that I had to go see Mom and Dad, where they are buried. Anna muttered something about how the trip would kill me and then she could just leave me there too, and I was a bit taken aback, but then she went off into a long harangue in her own language and afterwards began singing for some reason.

After lunch, a tuna sandwich I took just one half-hearted bite from, she calls from the kitchen sink as she is washing up, 'Okay, Jack. We go now. Okay?'

And off we go.

It's a beautiful spring day with the sun shining, but the wind has been sneaking through the cracks of the great thaw all week and that's why Anna has insisted on covering me in knitted blankets she found in some trunk in her sister's apartment in the west end of the city. Of course now I am sweating profusely and my hand slips every time I attempt to help her get us up the hill to the cemetery and I hear her tut behind me.

'Let me, Jack. You are too weak – a weak man.' Then she laughs.

A moment later, we are at the top of the hill and I can see the gates to the cemetery. Then we hit a bump in the sidewalk and I find myself face down in my own blood. On top of that, I feel like I am about to piss myself.

There is a holy commotion and a little girl appears in the corner of my one open eye: 'Hey, mister, are you dead or something?'

Then I hear a hoarser voice whose face I can't quite get in focus: 'Come on, Ronnie. Get away from the old man, he might have germs.'

'Fuck.' I am not sure if I say this out loud or not.

Anna is trying to get me back in the wheelchair and I feel like I weigh a ton. The hoarse voice is trying to help, breathing heavily in my ear. Ronnie takes a tissue out of her pocket and dabs my bloody brow.

'There you go, mister. I don't think you are gonna die, today.'

Easy for her to say.

'Fuck.'

Anna wants to go back home but I insist in carrying on. I have pissed myself, but if she knows this she doesn't say anything. Perhaps she is used to the stench. I am not, but I must visit Mom and Dad, though I have no idea why. She pushes me over the small grassy mounds toward the section where Mom and Dad lie, just rows apart, though separated by a squat and battered wall. We find Mom immediately, partly because of the huge monument just behind her, given over to the famous priest who helped build our church – Monsignor Corrigan. We never met him but heard too many sermons from old Father Mahoney about how giving money gets you closer to God. Mom would die again to know she somehow ended up lying so close to that man. Mom's grave has a simple marker with her name – Edna Gordon – in plain font on grey stone at ground level, nothing fancy. That's what she always said she wanted. But she wouldn't have fancied having her small marker overrun by grass and weeds. Anna helps me clear the area around the marker, so that you can read the name clearly, at least. We toss the roughage towards the holy monsignor. She probably thinking that she is showing him some great respect. I spit in his direction. She helps me back into my stinking chair and leaves me for a few moments. I try to clear my head. Why have I come? Maybe Anna is right. I should just stay here, die next to her and be buried right quickly.

I sit a long time then nod to Anna. 'Let's go home.'

'What about your father, Jack?'

'I don't know where he is,' I lie. 'Home.'

V

I have been dreaming of you again. Why won't you come and visit me? You know I am dying and don't have much longer. How cruel you are. I have sent you many letters, cards even, with pretty coloured flowers painted by some poor soul's mouth, but still you won't come. How you would play with that last sentence. You always had a good sense of the smutty, at least when we were behind closed doors. Do you remember the first time we slept together? Slept? you would say. I thought I had found the perfect place, there in your bed, where no questions were asked and no demands seemed too much. Every grasp was met with damp tenderness, every reach with wit and fleshy good will. I lay exhausted, guilt ridden too, I have to say, and then slowly your hand found my sex and methodically brought it back to life. God, could it be that there is a woman who understood this drive to get inside another, truly fuck them without regret or censure? But there was regret. There was censure.

Molly is here when I awaken after what seems like a long sleep. Why does she come here? If we had had children it would be easier to understand. Is she waiting for me to die? Or is she just curious to see how it happens? We were close once, so close. Now perhaps she is trying to understand what happens when some part of you – even if it is lost in the past – dies. Perhaps it helps you get ready.

The doctor tells me I am in a kind of remission, so the drug dosage has been cut back and I can sit up, talk and even hear close to normal. Molly is telling me about her latest trip to Latin America, where she is teaching English to Spanish-speaking children, helping them get jobs in the global economy. There was a time when I would have thought this admirable, something I might have joined her in. But today, despite feeling good, I think it is pointless. They are all going to die poor in their own countries anyway. Why lead them on? I decide not to mention this, change the subject.

'Do you remember why we broke up?' I ask, too bluntly.

Molly gives me that little half-smile which I always felt hid her feelings more than it revealed them. 'You wanted to fuck other women, as I recall.'

'Do you really think it was that simple?'

'Well, you do like to complicate things, Jack, but, yes, it was pretty much that simple.'

Suddenly it is quiet in the apartment. Anna has gone out for an hour by the lake. I think she is meeting her priest but she won't talk about it. Molly avoids looking at me, gazing out of the window where the sun is playing peek-a-boo with fluffy white clouds. She is sipping her milky tea. Outside, several streetcars go by, one after another, like there's been a delay along the line to the west of us.

'Why do you think I wanted to fuck those other women?'

Silence.

She turns her head away and I can't see her face but I think she is crying. I want to reach over to her and touch her arm, which hangs limply down the side of my one old comfy chair. I want to say I am sorry, not just for the fucking but for talking about it yet again. But I don't. It is too late.

... I have met Tessa for Mass during Easter holidays. Father Mahoney must be surprised to see us two teenagers, one fresh out of minor seminary, pressed together like sardines coming up the aisle for Communion. Tessa is flushed with the memory of our squeezing in a long drawn-out kiss in front of the church on our way in, and perhaps in anticipation of sneaking into her bed after Mass. Father Mahoney gives me a cold stare that speaks of the devil as we take Communion. I look away. Tessa is oblivious. Later, after wolfing down tea and cinnamon toast at her house, we go to Tessa's bedroom. Her mother, whose boyfriend is forced to sleep on a single bed in an old pantry when he doesn't get home to his own apartment, would kill us. Tessa keeps all her clothes on and tells me to do the same, but in moments I am on top of her, her lips enveloping my whole mouth, drawing me in. Before I know it, I have come, slowly, gently, into her hot mouth. I can't remember even pulling my jeans down ...

Anna is back now from her retreat with the women of her parish – led by her favourite young priest. She shows me a piece of paper. I am to read it when I feel well enough, she says. Anna is being very gentle today, brings me tea and toast. I sip the tea but ignore the toast. My stomach churns. Something has happened. I don't want to read the letter. It can only be bad news. I pretend to sleep and then fall off, immediately dreaming of you. But something is different.

. . . I arrive home late from work and you smell beer on my breath. I have been at a staff retreat, where we are compelled through silly games to get to know each other well, become a team by identifying our favourite colours, our deepest longings. Somehow you hate this corporate luxury. I explain that we are trying to help bring better service to the community, though I don't believe this, and you see through it. You are very unhappy in your work as a fashion journalist at that magazine. Your big butch editor yells at you when you get the colour of a starlet's eye shadow wrong. You take it out on me, heaving the pumpkin pie across the table at me. I pick it up and toss it into the bin under the kitchen sink and head out the door to the Anchor, the pseudo Brit pub around the corner that you hate because of all the old drooling men. At least that's what you say. You never mention the redhead behind the bar, who fancies me . . .

I can't remember what parts of that dream are true. I lift my hand to scratch my head and find the letter.

VI

Somehow I blame Mort, the priest who married Molly and me. During the wedding Mass at the old wooden Irish church in Scarborough, he preached this sermon on perfection, quoting Saint Paul saying we needed to be perfect just like the heavenly Father – in marriage. He knew Molly well. He didn't know me. He didn't know my mom and dad. I could feel my father's piercing glare through the back of my head as Mort went into his high-pitched homiletic extravagance. Dad was probably moments away from getting up and pounding little Mort, or me. Molly, he loved. But he thought she was too good for me. He was probably right. I am thinking all this, or half dreaming it as I lie in my living room hospital bed. I think Anna is listening to music in her room, my room. The doctor says my little blip of recovery is over, that there may be some more gentle times ahead, but he can't be sure. He didn't look particularly optimistic, kept a straight tanned face that somehow looks younger every time I see him (bastard). I am angry with him for this constant changing of his story. It's like he makes it up as he goes along. I am angry with Anna for being out of reach at this moment when I want some painkillers, some water, or her hand on my brow.

The letter sits where it has been for days, on my makeshift locker. It now has tea stains and something sticky on the envelope – I'm not sure what. I have decided the letter is from Molly, probably an explanation of why she hasn't been here for weeks, something to do with the 'fucking' conversation. Anna has already opened the envelope to make it easier for me to get at. Finally, I slip the letter out of the envelope. It is one page, signed in blue pen. It takes me a moment before I recognize Tessa's ornate letters. Tessa has written after all these years. Why Tessa? Why now?

'Jack, I don't suppose you remember that time I went away to Florida with the girls from school and you sent me that silly note about how much you missed me, body and soul, but you got real smutty at the end and I was so pissed off we

broke up for a while when I came back to Canada? Do you? For some reason now that I hear that you are dying, I keep thinking of that, what children we were trying to handle the beginnings of some kind of grown-up love in our new-found bodies, yours so straight and needy then, mine plump and growing into that desire that near destroyed us both before we went our own wretched ways. Well, it felt that way for a long time. There's been so many years since then, and while we only met that once in Greenwich Park on that freezing February day when we could practically see the few words we shared steaming from between our lips and you wore that ridiculous felt hat no one had the nerve to tell you made you look like a demented sea captain, I have thought of you from time to time with affection. It took a long time before I could even bring myself to utter your name without the words 'that fucking bastard' as some kind of adjectival phrase preceding it. But, as you can tell, I am over it now. That was meant as a joke, by the way, though I suspect you aren't in a joking mood. Sorry, I feel like I should write but I don't know what to say. I have to go now as the boys are coming to get their old mother and take me out for my birthday, a significant one, but you've surely not given it any thought. I am told there is a grandchild coming soon from the eldest son and his wife. I'm sorry that's something you won't get to enjoy. Such was your lifestyle. You probably want forgiveness for dumping me for Molly but, Jack, I can neither forgive nor forget, I just move on. I wish you well and hope the doctors in Toronto know how to keep the pain low for you. There's been enough pain for you, though most of it has been self-inflicted, I suspect. Sorry, I didn't want to end my note this way. I will not be able to come and visit but do know I send my very best. Tessa'.

I close my eyes, try to sleep, try to conjure up the kind of dream that will let me go off to sleep gently enough. It will not come. Tessa is right. We were children. It was crazy to think she would travel all this way to watch an old man slip away, an old man who has no connection to the hungry young man of half a century ago. Still . . .

I don't remember falling asleep but I am now awakened suddenly by an unholy racket coming from my kitchen. Pots and pans seem to be slamming against the linoleum floor and Anna is screaming. Then all goes quiet and I try to use my faint voice to call her.

'Anna, are you okay?'

I hear her talking but it is not to me.

'Of course I am sure, I am a woman, not a stupid priest. I know my body. My body is full of your business now, your baby priest, some kind of holy miracle you said would never happen. You lie, priest. You lie and now I die.'

Anna comes into the living room where I lie and sits on the old chair, puts her hands over her face, quietly weeping, her whole body shaking. After a long time, I try to say something consoling and she just lifts her hand towards me and I am silenced. An hour later she gets up and goes to the bedroom and closes the door. The drugs she has given me work slowly and I finally sleep, but there are no dreams, just a growing feeling of dread in the bottom of my stomach. Anna is in trouble.

VII

I am awake in the middle of the night, coughing, hacking so hard I can feel little parts of my insides, maybe my lungs, coming up with the phlegm and mucus. I cannot stop this rhythm of rocking with the roll of the cough; I am on a horse about to be bucked off; I think it is the end. Anna is nowhere in sight; you are off in some godforsaken ashram enjoying your spiritual orgasms; Tessa is with her new grandchild, a boy, I think; Molly – I must try to phone Molly, but I can't stop coughing long enough to hit the one number Anna says will bring Molly in an emergency. This is that emergency and – fuck – the floor feels cool but my head is lying in some dark sticky liquid. It smells like blood and urine. God, I have pissed myself. Where is Anna? Where is Molly?

… I am eight, and have been in bed for days, maybe weeks. Mom spells out the word for me but it makes no sense – bronchitis. I just know it hurts when I breathe, hurts more when I cough, and I can't stop coughing. I hear Dad and Mom yelling at each other downstairs, something about the new Chevy and a slut. I don't know what a slut is but it can't be good. Mom is crying now and Dad stomps around, opening then slamming the refrigerator door; it never sticks first time and he slams it again, cursing.

'Why the fuck did you buy this cheap thing? I told you if you wait a few weeks I'd get us a brand new one.'

'All our money goes on fixing up the cars when you get drunk. God knows how much you spend on those sluts of yours.'

'They're real women and show a hell of a lot more class than you ever do.'

'I'll show you class if you ever bring your pay cheque home.'

'Fucking likely.'

'Keep your voice down, you'll wake him.'

'Yes, your sensitive soul up there. You mollycoddling him, that's what's making him sick.'

'He's got bronchitis; you know that's what the doctor said.'

'Doc Wentworth doesn't know his ass from—'

I can't hear any more and soon enough start coughing again. I hear Dad on the stairs, the third one from the top creaking like it always does when he is on it with his bulky frame. I try to stop coughing but can't. In a moment my bedroom reeks of whiskey, but Dad silently gets me to open my mouth and fills it with a deep dollop of honey. He leaves me the spoon to lick and retreats downstairs. I fall into a deep restful sleep . . .

Anna is growing round and fat with child, and her mood is beginning to change. Now I think she wants this baby, this baby priest. She no longer talks about the father, the priest in his hand-tailored black suit and monkey collar. She hums quietly to herself while I sip tepid water and feel the skin shrivel over my ancient bones. It is as if I have given the fat I once carried to her so she can bear this child. In my dreams, you would laugh. In your dreams – and yes, you would be right. I would not have been able to make such a creation – not any more. But there was a time! Oh, there was a time! Still, Anna has some worries. Of course she doesn't tell me about them, but I hear her talking on that damn smarty phone she carries with her every minute of every day.

'I will have to go back to Philippines . . . Of course I will . . . No one will take care of me . . . the baby will be a Canadian baby but I will not have a job and will have to return to my poor country if I have no job . . . Looking after the baby will be my job . . . I try not to worry but. . .'

Anna's voice goes quiet or she shuts the door to my old room, I am not sure which. I drift off to sleep wondering who will look after me, or if she is presuming I will be dead before this baby priest comes into the world.

I was going to be one of those – priests – those men in brown robes, some brawny under the rough cloth with tough minds to match if you had them for Latin or Maths; some light as angels with feathered wings, who might have had girlish curves beneath Franciscan brown; we were too young to worry about the differences and looked up to them all when they entered chapel after us for special Masses, a river of brown-hooded men with bowed balding heads. I was going to be one of them; we all were – Jimmy, Mike and I. We wanted to get closer to God, feed the poor beggars in Toronto, build churches in the missions in far-off places like the Dominican Republic. We loved the incense and the old hymns and the way they made Jesus sound like a tough bugger who loved the odd one out. We loved the priest we called LBJ the best – the way in the good weather he walked us around the pond that was our hockey rink in the winter – 'Hail Mary, full of grace . . .' And the way he took us into the woods where an old friar by then long dead had carved out his own version of the Stations of the Cross on small wooden placards nailed to the fir trees. Jesus looked like a Franciscan friar and Mary Magdalene looked a bit like the seminary secretary, but on our good days we ignored that and prayed that somehow we would make it and become priests like LBJ – tall, straight, tough but fair in class and in the refectory, able to laugh a little at our nonsense. Jimmy and I would get chewed out for making too much noise on occasion (Mike never did) but LBJ knew we were kids away from home and suffering from homesickness and hormones. And I was going to be a priest. We all were. Jesus!

VIII

Anna has gone away. Molly is here for a few days. She says Anna just needs some time to rest. I wonder if there is some kind of problem with the baby but I am too weak to care. I can't keep food down. I sip apple juice and some kind of sugary water that Molly gets from the pharmacist. When she's not helping with my liquids, Molly sits reading in the corner, ignoring the squealing ambulances outside. It's like there is some kind of disaster taking place on the street below, but Molly settles in with her big fat book, adjusting the music on her little machine plugged into her right ear. It's probably some old folkie playing banjo or singing about poor single mothers. I think of Anna and hope the ambulances have nothing to do with her. I am worried about Anna.

I wake up from what seems like a long sleep, much more restful than usual. There's no sign of Molly. Her little music machine and book sit on the arm of the old chair. I think it is evening but it must be later as there is no traffic below. Perhaps Molly has gone to bed. My own bed is damp but I feel like I can get up, and so I slowly sit and then try swinging my legs around. I reach my left foot towards the little stool Anna sometimes sits at when she is cleaning me up and I think I have located it, but then my leg melts away and I go out cold. Everything goes black.

... Molly and I are huddled together in the back of rented truck, with a group of scrawny teenagers from our local church. We are driving around all night, going from congregation to congregation, saying prayers and singing folk mass music in each of them before moving on to the next. It is a Holy Thursday ritual we started a few years ago to keep the kids from just getting pissed and hanging around the beach all night, building bonfires, making out and creating too

much racket. I keep passing her shreds of my notebook with cheesy poems about pussy willows and cattails and love and sex, like I'm some kind of Lightfoot or Dylan. God. Somehow the words between us are always lyrical, important. But somehow there are always these long pauses, silences, between the words . . .

Anna is muttering something under her breath or I just can't hear her properly. On top of all the things happening to my now emaciated body, I am losing my hearing. I can still hear that constant ringing inside my hollow head but it just blocks out every other sound, especially first thing in the morning. As I get thinner, Anna gets fatter with child. She sweats and moans as she goes about keeping me clean, fed (though I eat little these days) and drinking, alas, just water or sometimes some kind of cheap ginger ale she picks up at the store on the corner across Queen Street. I listen closely and I think she is cursing me for taking so long to die, or she is talking to her priest, who, though he has apparently disappeared into his heart of darkness or South America, she talks to alternately in her first language then her broken English as if he were smack dab in the middle of the living room, which is now my dying room. Over the past few days while I have drifted between sleep and some kind of dreadful pissing wakefulness, Anna has hinted that she wants to talk to me about something, something important, she adds, something very important, Mr Jack. But I have not had the energy or the interest. Today, I think I will summon up the wherewithal to find out what is on her mind, though I'm convinced she wants more money or she is ready to quit because she can no longer bend over and pick up the drinking glass when I toss it on the floor in my feeble efforts to get her attention when I feel like I need another fix of the drugs that keep me from crying out to that elusive God. Where is he?

'Anna, do you still want to talk to me about that very important thing?'

'Maybe, old Jack, you can't see I am busy right now with your little lunch?'

'Yes, but I thought you were trying to talk to me just now again and I couldn't hear . . .'

'Not now, Mr Jack. Today I'm not happy, it's not a good time to talk to you.'

She is leaning over me now, sweat rolling off her brow, her now flabby arms reaching towards my heavy head, which hasn't moved since she helped me place it in the middle of the feathered pillow an hour ago. I think I see tears in her eyes too, but it could just be the perspiration that has flooded from her swollen round body since she has entered what I think are the final days of her pregnancy.

'Are you okay, Anna? Is there something you want to discuss with me? I'm sorry I was having a bad spell earlier and I didn't have the energy to talk. Now, I think I can. Tell me . . .'

Anna's hands go to her face and I hear a muted cry as she turns from me and walks quickly and laboriously to her room. I'm not sure what has happened to my lunch, though I am not hungry. I am also not sure what is happening to my primary caregiver. I only know that I have somehow made the situation worse. Is she going to walk out on me now? I don't know. Is there a problem with that priest's baby she is carrying? I don't know. I just want to sleep, and for a moment I think it will be better if she is gone when I awake. Then I can die here alone without any fuss. She is supposed to be my nurse and here I am having to worry about her. Curse her and her wretched little fucking priest. Curse Molly for going away on some godforsaken do-gooder exploit. Curse Tessa for that wicked little letter reminding me what a bastard of a young lover I was. And curse you, my great love, for running off to India with that knob-headed little phony holy man. Curse you all for abandoning me as I lie dying here alone. Will none of you stay with me for this short time? I planned a long life but that didn't work out so well. So now, thanks to the lack of medical miracles available to me, I am planning a short death. Just help me find the right dose. Where are you, you cowards? What the hell have I done to deserve this? Haven't I always stood by you, every damn one of you? God, please don't answer that question.

Have I been speaking these words aloud? Regardless, they leave me tired, full of despair and with a bitter taste in my mouth.

> *. . . God, but I am pissed. Been selling my soul and the virtues of the nuclear power industry to two journalists who are so poorly paid and easily impressed by my three-piece charcoal suit they have scribbled every little lie I can come up with. There are no dangers. There will never be an accident. Lake Ontario will remain pure and unsullied. Though I can't remember the last time I ever swam in that soup of dog shit and algae. Afterwards, the two budding scribes came back to the bar in my hotel room in your old Mennonite city in southern Ontario and we drank ourselves stupid. One was that silly Brit with the luscious dark eyes who couldn't stop flirting with every man at least six foot tall, who always seemed to love you for the first five minutes or until her second drink arrived and then you could follow those black pools as they wandered around the room while you seemed to disappear. It took me a while to figure out that she fancied the reporter from the local radio station and even I had to admit that he had that quiet, wry way of telling a tale that gets women somewhere in the solar plexus, or at least that's what you used to say. Anyways, wry guy, who was drinking whiskey greedily was craftily shifting the conversation further and further afield from the nuclear nonsense that was paying*

my considerable bar bill and soon the two of them were tête-à-tête talking about their respective editors who were famously fucking each other for the betterment of local journalism. Even I, drunk as I was on Vancouver red beer could tell that I was standing in the way of some kind of nuclear or sexual fusion. So, I fucked off and drove to the plaza near your place, parked my car and called you on the pay phone near that little restaurant with the long red bar and high wooden stools, where the slim grey-haired waitress used to eye me suspiciously when I entered on my own and even more suspiciously when I left with you, our faces flushed from the smutty talk in our back booth and your lipstick somehow managing to find its way on to my tie. Only after I hung up on you did I see the police officers eyeing me from the patrol car a few parking lanes away from my car and, pissed as I was, I headed for the street like I'd never seen the silver sports car I so fancied, when they called me over and I held my beer breath while they grilled me on why I was leaving the car in the lot, it being private property. I said I had to go visit a friend around the corner and that I would be back to get it later. They knew I was pissed and were dying to get me to slip into the front seat and turn the key so they could start flashing their red lights and take me in for driving under the influence. See you, I said, and made my way to yours, praying to that God again. Then I dragged you back to drive my car to your little condo, the ticky-tacky box you called it, but for me it was so often, in those days of terror and titillation, my refuge from confusion, somewhere to forget everything but your mouth swallowing my cock, my cum, my desire. Except today you slipped on the ice and cracked your head and I just charged ahead telling you to get up because we had to get my car before the cops towed it. You yelled at me, screamed at me and I came back and pressed my tissue against that wound and wondered why your blood was black, not red . . .

IX

Anna is back fussing with my meds and my sheets and pillow. It's like she wants to wake me up, to talk to me. My bed is dry and it is too soon to get my surge of sweet relief from Big Pharma. She wants to talk but won't look me in the eye. I try to pull myself out of this groggy dream and speak to her. Either she didn't hear me or the words didn't actually come out of my mouth, stayed somehow in my head, in my imagination. I try again.

'What is happening to you, Anna? Do you need to talk to me?'

Silence.

'Can you hand me my glass of water, please?'

Anna lumbers closer to the side of the bed where I have curled up against the demons. Her due date can't be far off but I have lost track of how long before she gives birth and flees this work she has come to hate. She hopes I will be dead before the child arrives. She places the water bottle in my hand. Looks down on me with a mix of pity and pain. She opens her little round mouth to say something but then appears to change her mind, turns away, yet again.

'Just sit here a moment,' I try.

'Too busy to just talk, Jack. You are full-time work without your nonsense talk.'

As she speaks, a tiny tear forms in her left eye and she tries to wipe it away with her plastic-gloved hand. But she doesn't move.

'How are you doing? How are plans for the baby going?' I ask.

Then I break into a cough and she takes the water from me until I stop and then hands it back and helps me take a long gulp.

'I must go back to my country.'

I don't know how to respond to Anna's cry. My eyes are heavy and I drift into deeply medicated sleep.

... It is our last night of seminary life. Mike, Jimmy and I slip out of our beds in the senior dorm at precisely midnight. Jimmy is wearing those garish orange pyjamas, Mike and I manage to find our robes to go over our more understated nightwear. We sneak down the main stairs, tiptoe past the door to the monastic enclosure. We have never been behind those doors in four years here and this is not the time to enter, or waken the priests and brothers. A few more steps down the stairs and we are in the long corridor to the main doors. We open the door as quietly as we can and run as fast as our slippers can carry us to the little brown house that up until a year ago was the home of our caretakers, Cornelius and Maria. Now it is empty and Jimmy has stashed some altar wine and potato chips there – as well as his transistor radio.

When we first arrived at Saint Francis Seminary we were as holy as the priests and brothers themselves, solemn during Mass, conscientious in our studies, disciplined. Jimmy was naturally bright and finished his work first, then read Steinbeck and the Canadian spy story on Igor Gouzenko from our little well-stocked library down the corridor from our classroom. Mike worried his way through every course, studied like a fiend, and only relaxed when his straight A's were posted on the bulletin board near the first-floor locker room. I was up and down, doing well in French and English but bombing in the Sciences and Math. Latin was a struggle. But I led the choir once the holy brother who had led us had a breakdown and refused to take charge any more. In the beginning we were all going to be priests but as the reality of a life without girls, women, sex became brutally clear to us, we began to lose, not just our vocation to the priesthood, but our love of Mother Church. I tried to leave once but my father said I needed to stay until the end of the year, then decide. He told me to masturbate, that sex was over-rated. He told me to study. His sermon didn't help. For weeks I was sick in bed and the priests were ready to send me home, but I recovered and agreed to stay on.

We drink bitter altar wine until three in the morning, the salt and vinegar chips keep us going back to the holy bottle for more, but it fails to quench. We talk about our plans for next year, the girls we are going to finally chase. We laugh about this, bitter laughs after four years of sexual frustration. Jimmy wants to start a business, Mike will be an accountant. I have no clue but say I want to write novels. We all laugh. Mike is nervous. There is no studying for this kind of adventure. If we are caught we will lose our chance to graduate and will have to repeat back in the city. Mike shushes us, thinks he hears somebody. There is a long moment when we can only hear the crickets outside the window, and then LBJ walks through the door. He is dressed in a nightgown, looking very un-Franciscan. He says nothing. He doesn't have to. He motions toward the door with his long scholarly neck. We run back to our dorm. The next morning nothing is said. Our parents arrive one by one and we leave, certain we will never return . . .

X

When I wake up, Anna is no longer there. But the doctor (bastard) appears from the small bathroom, looking over his glasses at me. He can't wait for me to die. I know this for sure. He manages a wan smile and starts to speak then simply chuckles to himself, walks away to the kitchen, returning moments later with a glass of water and some kind of blue pill.

I want to joke that it is perhaps something to give me an erection but can't get the words out.

'Your blood work is not good,' he says without the smile, looking almost sympathetic, though that makes him appear ridiculous to me. Maybe it is my prejudice against him. He is only ever the bearer of bad news. He doesn't disappoint.

'I fear your time is coming, my friend.'

I blanch at that word – friend.

'Jack, you need to make your peace – with family, friends, God, whoever. You do not have long, I'm sorry to say.'

And he does look sorry.

Not as sorry as me.

... Mom and Dad are both dying at the same time, in the same house, in the same bed. It didn't happen that way, but no mind. This is what I see, standing over the bed, the sweet stench of death in my lungs. Mom grabs me by the shirt collar, looking directly at me, through me. Her eyes are urgent, her words desperate.

'You promised to bring the gun. Where is the gun? Bring the gun. I want to go. You said you would help.'

She collapses, letting go of my shirt, and falls into a deep sleep, not quite death but close enough for me to turn to Dad on the other side of the blood-drenched bed. He moans inarticulately and blood continues to flood all around him. Soon he begins swallowing the blood and I can hear him coughing, choking, crying ...

Anna is back. I need to talk to her. She has been crying, her eyes deep ponds of tears as she brings me more water and another blue pill. No jokes from me. I don't even mention her weeping. I have a question to ask.

'Can you find me a priest?'

She throws her arms up into the air, laughs bitterly. 'No.'

'Yes, I am dying ...'

'I know. You are taking your time dying, though ...'

Somehow we both manage a laugh, barely audible.

I try again. 'I need to see a priest, a particular priest, a Franciscan from many years ago.'

'He's probably dead.'

This sucks the breath right out of me. I can't believe what Anna has said, and yet she is probably right.

There is a long pause. I catch my breath.

'Still, I need to try.'

I point to the dresser with my old address books and she goes hunting, happy, it seems, to have a project, other than wiping up my vomit. She pulls up the loose trousers she now wears around her expanding waist and moves towards the dresser, spends a few minutes looking through the ringed books, finally letting out a small sigh of recognition. I manage to grab hold of the little microphone attached to the little whirling machine that now takes my notes for me and whisper all this into it, hoping Anna remembers to type it out. I sometimes wonder if she remembers to do this for me even though she has promised many times. I also wonder what she might be leaving out, something I could never do myself.

'I will phone. You sleep now.'

... All my dreams are jumbles now. Perhaps they always have been. We sneak away from our legitimate beds to that bed and breakfast near the Shakespearean theatre, the bliss of this bed that we drenched in our sweat and cum between the matinee and the evening performance, the Lear that you found so shocking in its austere décor that you somehow felt it lost its own plot. I escape to the toilet at the interval only to find it somehow full of those green garbage bags you once sent to my apartment, all my belongings, clothes, tapes, books with a note that said: 'If you can't make up your own

mind, I will make it up for you. Fuck off now.' I sit on the bathroom floor looking among the bags for God knows what...

XI

Anna touches my shoulder.

'You are talking like a crazy man in your sleep. I need to give you this drink, this pill. I phoned your priest. This LBJ priest is dead. They are sending another brown Franciscan.' She laughs. 'This one is alive. Father Michael.'

I don't laugh. I don't cry. I roll over and fall back to sleep. This time there are no dreams. It is as if I have no strength even for dreams. I wonder where you are now. But somehow I know you are gone forever and will not come to see me one more time. My account is overdrawn by many years. I want to tell Anna to forget about this Father Michael, probably some young clean-shaven priest from Eastern Europe, full of righteous holiness, someone who won't have a clue about the kind of life I have lived, someone who will judge me as harshly as I am today judging myself. I want to tell Anna to forget it, but I can only turn away in shame. I hear someone crying but I am not sure if it is Anna or myself.

When I awake, my whole body is in pain and even the drip they have me on now does little to blunt it. I am melting away in my bed in this apartment. I think I hear the streetcars clipping along Queen Street but they are a million miles away. I hear voices and I am sure Molly is talking to Anna, who is crying, but I open my eyes and there is no one there. I close them again.

Another nudge on my shoulder and I want to hit out in response but nothing moves, not even my eyelids. Then water touches my lips, a facecloth washes over my scalp and forehead, then cleans my eyes, and I can see Anna standing beside a wizened little man in brown. It is not LBJ but there is something familiar about him, his face, perhaps, or maybe just his brown habit. He speaks softly and I can barely make out his words. Anna tells him to move closer.

'It's been such a long time . . .'

'You're not LBJ . . .'

'He's in heaven now.'

I want to laugh but something tells me not to.

'Did you know him?'

'Of course. Don't you remember me?'

My brain is doing a kind of mathematics through a haze of drugs, pain, years, and memory lapses. There is a long silence then a short-circuit explosion occurs in my foggy head. Mike, Mike from Saint Francis Seminary. We have two-thirds of the unholy trinity from the seminary. I wish I could say this but utter something less divine.

'Fuck.'

He ignores this.

I see it then, the same worried look on his now-wrinkled face. He had a great blond head of hair but is now completely bald. His eyes look directly at me as they always did those years ago when we were too young to articulate our fears of a life of order in the Roman Catholic Church. Somehow now they offer something else – wisdom, understanding. But it could just be that he is wearing brotherly brown. I want to ask him about this but he continues talking solemnly.

'I'm Brother Michael now, not a priest. I was married forty years then Marni passed away and they took me back. Four grown kids and they still took me back. The three daughters are happy, but my son, well, let's just say he is adjusting . . . I'm running a recruitment programme, trying to get older men to join us in God's work, keeping the order, what is it they say "sustainable" . . .'

I see a joke and reach for it.

'Count me in.'

Brother Michael smiles though I am not sure he knows what I said. My voice won't carry far enough. Anna pushes him closer towards me and hands him something, the microphone?

'Why did you want to talk to LBJ now?'

'I'm dying,' I cry.

'I understand.'

'I think I need to know . . . need to understand . . . how badly I've fucked . . . messed it up, my life. Safe to say the good Franciscans wouldn't let me back in.'

He laughs this time.

'I'm not sure what I can do. I can't hear your Confession. But we can talk.'

I hadn't actually considered Confession and this surprises me. I need a moment before I continue down this road.

'How's Jimmy? Has anyone heard from him? I lost track. I lost track of so many of the guys, of so many things . . .'

'I'm afraid I don't know what happened to Jimmy either. He was one smart fellow, would have made a great priest. Except for the God part. He'd given that up by the time we all left.'

'Tell me about God,' I whisper.

'Why don't you tell me?'

I take a long breath. 'Trouble is I keep changing my mind – creator, source of love one day; harsh judge the next . . .'

'Perhaps they are both true.'

'I see why they let you back in.'

We both laugh quietly. Anna hovers in the background, then brings water and another blue pill.

Brother Michael looks at his watch, the smile disappearing from his face.

'Or, there is no God at all, just a mythical joke . . .'

Brother Michael ignores this.

'Are you looking for forgiveness? God forgives, you know.

You just need to ask for it then change your ways. You don't need a priest or brother for that ...'

'That's not what they used to teach us.'

'Things have changed.'

'Really?'

'Well, they *are* changing.'

'Sure.'

XII

Anna has gone back into the kitchen and is fussing with pots and pans and maybe crying again.

Brother Michael looks towards the kitchen then turns back and leans in closer to me, so I won't miss his words. 'Let's talk about Anna.'

I'm shocked. 'What?'

'Anna needs your help. There's something you can do for her ...'

Brother Michael speaks for what seems like a long time. I can't believe what I am hearing. Brother Michael came to see me but now he wants to talk about Anna. I can help Anna. It's me that's bloody dying, not Anna. But suddenly, the mathematics are working their way through my brain again. I try to sit up and Brother Michael holds me back. I need to rest, think, maybe pray.

XIII

Brother Michael leaves and I turn away in my bed of sweat and stale breath and the flaked skin I am shedding every day like a snake withering away after too many hot summers in the desert. I am awake, barely, but I don't want to see Anna just now and I don't want her talking to me. I hear her radio playing music from her country and wonder if that is her humming along or if it is part of the recording. Soon it fades and I fall asleep.

For once there is no dreaming, at least none that I can remember. I am weak, very tired still, yet can feel a new kind of strength; perhaps it will get me through the day. I ask Anna to phone Brother Michael and then I whisper into Anna's smarty phone to him.

'I get it. I get it. I will do it.'

Brother Michael responds approvingly but his words are sharp along the line. 'Do this because it is a good thing to do. It doesn't buy you an eternity of good dreams.'

XIV

I roll over and go back to sleep, this time fitfully but do not waken up for almost twenty-four hours.

The next morning Anna sings in the kitchen, brings me tea and another pill. She smiles, touches my head and whispers. I am weak, very weak. I can barely breathe, see or hear.

'It won't be long now,' she promises.

... There is a wedding at the beach just a few steps from my apartment, a skeletal man in a wheelchair and a fat bride, but in this day and age no one blinks an eye at such a sight. She is beautiful, dark, brooding, but in her heart she knows she will be fine. She can stay in this country, raise her child in a good neighbourhood, in a small but pleasant apartment. She will have an adequate pension to help with expenses, insurance money and a brother in a brown habit who has promised to be the child's godfather. She will visit the graveyard where Mom and Dad lie rows apart, have her

baby baptized in the church where I once served Mass. She will write to you, to Molly, to Tessa and tell you all about the last days. And she will spare no details for she promised only to speak the truth. And she says she will tell her child about me, even about the warts on my backside. She laughs about this. But while she has cleaned up my vomit and piss and shit for these past months, she vows not to clean up my story, all she has witnessed and all that she has typed about on these pages. She has nursed me all these months and in this last station holds me close, trusts me in such a way as to say, even broken like this, perhaps you're okay. I struggle to believe her, and no wonder. I remember Brother Michael's warning, but I still ask myself, if there is a God, might she too accept such an imperfect offering . . .

Playing Catch

Gripping the tight lace that winds its way around the hardball, Eric tossed it into his weathered Wilson.

*

To the slightly gimpy forty-year-old, it was a magical sound that brought back memories of the first fresh smack of a baseball hitting a mitt too many summers ago.

Partly it was the sound, a loud pure smack; partly it was the rhythm – smack, two, three, four; smack, two, three, four – that took him back.

He tossed the ball into the glove again. But that was just the warm-up. The real smack, the smack that sounded like cracking firewood in the early fall; the real rhythm, the rhythm of perfect ocean waves rolling against a beach head that was catch. Two guys tossing for all they're worth, back and forth, catching nonchalantly and firing it back like the World Series is on the line.

*

The first time Eric played catch with his dad, he was five. He hadn't quite learned to squeeze the ball and it squirted from his tiny spanking new glove and bopped him right under his right eye. The shiner was a family conversation piece for ages.

But the games of catch continued. And over the years they developed a ritual all their own. It was a special time of bonding, father to son, man to man, fathering son to failing father. Something happened when they would gather ball and glove and meet behind the battered shed near the elm in the backyard, something only a father and son can understand.

*

When he was ten, Eric wanted to count every throw; he would do it loud as he could, bellowing louder as the numbers got higher, muttering under his breath if he dropped the ball, recovering quickly and starting the count over.

Back and forth, the ball would fly, father to son, son to father – wind up, smack; wind up, smack. The rhythm was music to their ears, balm to their aching bodies, food for their souls. Wind up, smack; wind up, smack; wind up, smack. Rarely did they drop the ball. They were a beautiful sight, with the wind whipping through their hair and the sun filling their cheeks with reddish health.

And something else was happening, something almost mystical.

It soon became clear to father and son – though they never spoke of it – that this was a holy time, a time of suspended animation, suspended anger, suspended pain; and the lawn, sacred ground. No matter how angry they were with each other five minutes before, no words of anger were exchanged when they were throwing the baseball back and forth.

*

When he was twelve, Eric had a temper. The least little thing could set him off. Randy, the kid down the street, borrowed his bicycle one time and forgot to bring it back from where he had gingerly laid it outside the doughnut store downtown. Eric flew into a fit, kicking everything he could find in the yard – laundry basket, clothes pins, the cat. His dad was not happy and grounded him for two days, and, as if to add insult to injury, took away all biking privileges.

Father and son could barely speak to each other for days without getting into a major battle, Eric maintaining he had a right to be angry, his father warning him to find a better way to express it. They glared at each other over the serene mound of mashed potatoes Mom had placed as a kind of peace offering onto the Thanksgiving table.

After stuffing himself with turkey and mashed potatoes, Eric walked silently to the hall cupboard and picked up his left-handed ball glove, slipped his hand into it and quickly grabbed the hardball he got for Christmas the year before. He opened the creaky back door and slipped out into the last vestiges of early evening light.

A few minutes later, his father joined him down under the elm. Silently, rhythmically, the ball would arc its way from glove to glove: smack, two, three, four; smack, two, three, four; smack, two, three, four.

For now, everything was all right between them; for now, he could do no wrong; his father was gentle, understanding. Smack, two, three, four; smack, two, three, four; smack, two, three, four.

It wasn't as if no words were spoken. They congratulated each other when they caught the tough ones that looked like they would sail on down toward the creek.

'Good one.'

They commiserated when the easy ones slipped from their grasp.

'Nice try.'

But mostly they were quiet, admiring the arc of the ball, the smack in the glove, the grip, the feel. Sometimes they pitched to each other, threw grounders or pop flies, but mostly it was just plain catch. Smack, two, three, four; smack, two, three, four.

Eric realized something beautiful was happening, something he would never be able to articulate. And he wondered if he and his father should spend their lives just playing catch. That way there would be no anger, no pain.

But it wasn't to be.

*

When Eric was 16, he grew his hair long and put away his ball and glove. There were constant battles with his father about his hair, late nights and the guys (and girls) he was hanging around with. Once, when he stayed out all night at the beach with his girlfriend, Sara, his father had a fit. There was yelling and screaming and a kitchen fight during which a table was thrown, tears shed. Nobody remembers who threw what but everyone recalls there was a mini-ice age before the two six-footers took the now-battered gloves from the cardboard box in the front hall cupboard.

Silently they made their way down the path towards the shade of the elm. Eric pulled a tattered Yankee ball cap over his grimy locks. He gripped the stitching, wheeled back and let it fly with all his might. And then it started: smack, two, three, four. Smack, two, three, four. Few words were spoken. It was more like a silent ceasefire, punctuated only with the smack and whirl of two grown men playing a boy's game. Wind up, smack; wind up, smack; wind up, smack.

*

When he graduated from college, Eric had several job opportunities but eschewed them all to work in a downtown drop-in centre that welcomed draft resisters from the States. As if that wasn't enough for his blue-chip Tory father, Eric began bringing the stringy-haired hippies to the house for supper and closeting himself with them afterwards in his room. His father swore he could smell something more than just the political flavour of the day wafting from Eric's room, but Eric, who kept the door locked during these clandestine sessions, protested his innocence.

The political organizing led to long-winded diatribes in the left-wing press, marches on the US consulate, angry words on the steps of the Legislature and an ultimatum for Eric.

'Cool it or find your own pad,' his father ordered with just enough mockery to spark Eric's always volatile temper. Doors were slammed, a foot went through a wall and Eric remembers screaming 'fascist' at the top of his lungs.

On the day he gathered up his tattered belongings to start a new life with the mini-skirted artist he met on the Queen Street streetcar, Eric discovered his childhood baseball mitt beneath a stack of accounting textbooks in the basement crawl space. He slipped it on and began tossing the bruised ball into the old glove: smack, two, three, four; smack, two, three, four. Within minutes he felt transformed into that young lad of five, a badge of honour beneath his eye, but loved, valued.

He staggered outside, ignoring for now the chatter of his mother and the tie-dyed girlfriend in the kitchen, and made his way to the spot in the backyard where the celebrated games of catch took place. The bank executive pulled the ball from his glove and threw it back: wind up, smack; wind up, smack; wind up, smack. They were playing catch again. Silently. As the ball whirred its way from glove to glove, man to man, it was as if they were saying that, despite political differences, hair, smoke, suits, they were father and son and that's all that really mattered.

No one said a word a few minutes later as Eric got into the passenger seat of the Volkswagen van and gave the peace sign to his crying mother. Eric's girlfriend put the van in gear and they pulled away.

*

Time passed and the girl became Eric's wife and then a mature artist who realized she was never going to become rich and famous attached to a failed accountant in a backwater town. She left on a 747 for Paris on a beautiful spring day. Eric was angry and confused. He went to see his mother and father, hoping for a warm bowl of soup and a friendly ear but instead ran into a hailstorm of abuse from his father.

'You were the cause of that marriage going down the drain. No ambition. That girl wanted the good things in life and you gave her this backward town and that basement business of yours. You should have gone out and made something of yourself.'

Eric, now in his 30s, felt like he did the time Tommy Banks took the hockey stick to his backside after a practice for the church league twenty years ago: pummelled, abused. He could barely get his breath, let alone respond to this assault on his dignity. He left the living room of his parents' house and stepped on to the front porch. He was too old to put his foot through the new colour television, which is what he really wanted to do. He sat down in his miserable tears and pain and closed his eyes.

After what seemed like a very long time, he heard the front door open and a dull thud against the floor by his feet. He opened his eyes. No one was there, but his slightly mangled baseball glove lay at his feet. He wasn't sure he could do it. There comes a time when the bitter words of men won't be healed by the games of boys. He kicked the glove off the porch and stormed down the steps to his rusting Toyota. He was just about to get into the car when he heard it: smack, two, three, four; smack, two, three, four. It wasn't real catch but the sound of a strong man pounding a ball into his glove, readying himself for catch.

Slowly, reluctantly, Eric trudged to the backyard. Beneath the old elm stood the father he had hated with all his heart just minutes ago. He was slower of foot now but could still toss like Nolan Ryan. Eric held out his glove and the ball hit it with a smack. He pulled it out of his glove like it was a hand grenade and he a crazed terrorist. Wind up, smack; wind up, smack; wind up, smack. They were playing catch again, after all those years. Harsh words disappeared, failed marriages evaporated. No more anger, no more pain. Just the fragile love of two men strung across the arc of a baseball: smack, two, three, four; smack, two, three, four; smack, two, three, four.

Through his own blurred eyes, Eric thought he could see tears in his father's eyes for the first time in his life.

*

Soon after, Eric moved to another city some miles away and his trips home were infrequent. He got married and had a baby boy he and his wife called Jason. One frigid winter night Eric received a phone call from his mother. His father was in the hospital. It was his heart. It didn't look good. Would he come home right away? The icy roads were like an Olympic toboggan run and the fog gave the journey a dream-like quality but Eric could not turn back. He fixed his eyes on the transport truck in front of him and kept his hands firmly clenched on the wheel. Twelve hours later, he turned into the hospital in his home town.

He met his mother in the intensive care waiting room. She hugged him damply, pressed a package into his hands and steered him to his father's bed. She left them alone. His father was barely conscious. Eric took his hand and caressed it gently. The old man in the bed didn't look like his father. It was like someone had reached in and scooped out his heart and soul and left this shell of a man. Eric wanted to tell him that, despite everything, he loved him. But his sobbing kept the right words from coming. He opened the package and found a baseball and two old ball gloves.

'Jesus,' he gasped. 'What the hell does she expect?'

Eric placed his father's glove on the old man's blue-veined left hand, put on his own glove and gripped the ball. He didn't throw it but did a kind of simulated wind-up and gently smacked it into his father's glove. A whispering nurse whisked him out. He got halfway across the room when he heard something hit the floor. He couldn't believe his eyes. He looked over at his father and saw a faint smile across his face. Eric picked up the baseball and left the room.

The next morning Eric's father died, the same smile on his face, the battered ball glove on his hand.

*

Gripping the tight lace that winds its way around the hardball, Eric tossed it into his weathered Wilson.

'Jason,' he called. 'It's time to learn how to play catch.'

The boy took his father's hand and crossed the street to the green belt. Eric placed the spanking new glove on his son's hand. He squatted in front of the lad and whispered in hushed tones. 'Never forget this: I love you. No matter how mad I get, no matter what you do. Even if I refuse to say it, I love you. But when we are playing catch, that's a special time of love between you and me. Okay?'

Jason peered into his father's glistening eyes and responded in his direct five-year-old's way. 'Dad, can we play catch now?'

The Bottle Man

I first encountered the Bottle Man in 1955 when a crowd of neighbours from our street in the shadow of the stately clock tower gathered in front of Number 38 to watch the blood and pus ooze from Jimmy C's head wound.

Jimmy C had been tossing chestnuts at the immigrants across the road when he eased out past a parked car to get a better shot and found himself staring into the headlights of the East End Market truck.

The East End Market driver never had a chance to stop.

Cassidy, the firefighter who worked under the clock tower, was one of the first on the scene. He helped comfort Jimmy C and then knelt and mouthed a silent prayer. We all knew Jimmy C wasn't going to make it.

He was a fragile little thing and no one could figure out why he was throwing chestnuts at the new kids.

Most of the neighbourhood was there. It was a late summer afternoon and all the kids were home from school. Our dads were starting to make their way up the street in the Chevrolets and Pontiacs, honking to halt the games of catch or hide and seek that were constantly starting then stopping throughout the lazy summer.

My best friend Tucker and I probably had the best view of Jimmy C as he lay on the road. We heard this ghostly moaning coming from Jimmy C's motionless body. Then suddenly it stopped like it was hushed by some power we couldn't see.

We were silent for a few moments, then Tuck poked me in the ribs and pointed over at the East End Market driver, who was leaning on his green blood-splattered truck puking up something awful. We were getting an eyeful of east-end life that afternoon and weren't going to let each other miss one little detail.

'See that, Jay,' Tuck said.

'Yeah, I see it, Tuck. Just like my brother the time the old man made him smoke a whole cigar. Cured him for life.'

'Here comes the guys.'

The spectacle had drawn Carruthers, the skinniest kid in the neighbourhood, Ralph, who never stopped talking, and Beaut, the rich kid everyone wanted as best friend.

'Hey, you guys,' Tuck said. 'We were here first. The driver just barfed. We think Jimmy C is a goner.'

While Tuck continued his play-by-play, I turned to watch the crowd gather. That was when I first saw him – the Bottle Man. Or at least that was what we came to call him. We never bothered to find out his real name.

The Bottle Man looked like he was in his sixties even back then, with his wildly greased grey hair pointing out in a million different directions, his eyebrows arched towards each other. He was unshaven, smelled like a sewer and wore clothes that looked like Sally Ann rejects. The Bottle Man pushed this old grocery cart full of empty bottles: pop, beer, wine, whiskey, you name it. His gnarled fingers gripped the rusting cart like he was hanging on to his most prized possession.

The Bottle Man must have known Jimmy C. He shoved his cart between Ralph and Beaut to get a better look as Cassidy and the ambulance attendants gingerly lifted Jimmy C's corpse on to the stretcher and slid it into the back of the ambulance.

'Jesus,' the Bottle Man hissed in that wheezy way he had of taking breath and speaking at the same time. 'I knew that guy.'

The next thing I knew, the Bottle Man had disappeared up the street. We would learn later he had a way of doing that – showing up out of nowhere then all of a sudden disappearing.

It might have been the way he gripped the cart, the smell of him or how he fixed his stare on poor Jimmy C that day, I didn't know. I just somehow figured I would be seeing a lot more of him.

It turned out I was right.

The Bottle Man had a habit of appearing at many of the neighbourhood informal gatherings.

For instance, the first time we ever saw a woman wearing a bikini at the beach, the Bottle Man showed up. It was Rusty's mom. Rusty's family lived two streets over. His mom was beautiful, long-legged with red hair and a flat tummy. On this day, she shocked the neighbourhood by wearing this little polka-dotted bikini, just like in the song. A huge crowd had gathered that day too, Most of us were just standing there gawking. Some older guys were making strange sounds with their mouths but Rusty's mom was ignoring them, ignoring all of us.

The Bottle Man was in the thick of it. Most of the neighbours knew him by then. He started yelling at Rusty's mom, telling her she was causing a disturbance and that she was going to burn in hell, or at least get a nasty sunburn. We didn't know whether to laugh or cry.

The Bottle Man appeared too the day the cops came to give us hell for climbing all over the garages in the laneway behind our street. We were jumping from garage to garage, hooting and hollering like a pack of banshees. Neighbours peered from behind their curtains, but we played on. We figured Frampton called the cops. Frampton always called the cops. Suddenly the Bottle Man showed up. It was late afternoon on a Thanksgiving weekend and the grocery cart was extra full. The cops eyed him suspiciously but they were too busy giving us the third degree.

Then the Bottle Man started yelling at us. 'You boys are in trouble. These police officers will take you away and you'll never see your families again. You boys are in deep trouble.'

He had trouble getting his breath and all those words out at the same time. He looked worse than usual that day. His baggy pants were ripped, his shirt soiled and his breath was so foul, it sent us reeling. His eyes bugged out, lending him a kind of demonic stare. Something had taken a hold of him, that's for sure. We had no idea.

'Move along, old timer,' Maitland, the biggest cop, said, pointing towards the adjoining lane. I think he'd run into the Bottle Man a few times before. 'Move along now, mister.'

'Don't tell me what to do, I know your father. He's a religious man.'

The Bottle Man shouted something else over his shoulder but we couldn't make it out. Maitland's lecture on private property had resumed. We were in trouble but not the kind the Bottle Man imagined.

Another time we were putting up the lights over at Corpus Christi Church's tennis courts, across from the racetrack. The Catholic Youth Organization wanted to go big time, play some night games. Cassidy climbed the poles to do that last bit of wiring and we all craned our necks to watch him work. It scared the crap out of me. I swore then and there I'd never go working for the hydro or anything where I had to climb that high.

Out of the blue, the Bottle Man turned up yet again. He had that knack. He started screaming at Cassidy really loud, giving him proper hell. 'Those lights are going to disturb the neighbours, change the whole darn neighbourhood. Get off the pole, man. You're going to fall if you don't watch out. Get down from there.'

Tuck's old man and Beaut's mom were there and they grabbed a hold of the Bottle Man's grocery cart and shoved it toward Queen Street. The Bottle Man never let go. He just kept yelling all kinds of nonsense, spitting all over his grimy chin and twisting his neck backwards to let out one more rant.

‘Somebody ought to do something about that guy,’ Tuck said to me. ‘The Bottle Man’s a danger. He could have got Cassidy killed.’

‘I don’t know,’ I said. ‘He doesn’t do much harm. He’s just the Bottle Man. That’s what he does. Raise some shit, disappear. Show up again; raise some shit, disappear.’

‘He’s crazy,’ Tuck shrugged. ‘A real crazy guy.’

One time we were playing ball hockey on the street when the Bottle Man nearly did get Tuck killed. Ball hockey was kind of our religion when we were kids. We spent more time on the street firing frozen tennis balls at makeshift snow nets than we did serving Mass for Father Thomas, and that was saying something. We were on the street all day, every Saturday, right after church on Sunday, and all through the Christmas and Easter holidays.

I was always Billy Harris, Number 15 for the Toronto Maple Leafs. He was slight, like me, and could weave in and out of the clutches of the opponents like no other National Hockey League player in those days when there were only six teams. Those were the days.

So the Bottle Man showed up during one of the all-day tournaments we organized against the kids from Kip Avenue. We were winning the game but the Bottle Man somehow thought he knew how to improve our play.

He started bellowing at Tuck, our goalkeeper, trying to get him to change his stance.

‘Stand up, boy. Stand up. They’re going to score over your shoulder. That’s not the way to play goal. Don’t you watch the Leafs on Hockey Night in Canada? Stand up.’

Tuck had had enough. He took his goal stick and charged right at the Bottle Man. Beaut and I managed to get between them for a moment, but eventually Tuck overpowered us and chased the Bottle Man all the way down our street to the old Borisko Brothers Warehouse in the laneway near the fire hall.

Then the Bottle Man suddenly turned around and charged right back at Tuck, ramming his now-empty grocery cart right into Tuck's middle. Tuck doubled over in pain, gasping for breath, all the while cursing the Bottle Man's family, wherever they were, for letting him wander the streets the way he did. It was grim.

Just then, one of the yellow Borisko Brothers trucks came out of the loading docks. We all moved out of the way. Tuck was bent over and didn't see it coming. The Borisko driver saw Tuck at the last second and swerved to miss him. But the truck just grazed his left shoulder and Tuck was down.

And he was out for six weeks with a broken shoulder.

The Bottle Man, meanwhile, had disappeared.

The cops found him a few days later, apparently sleeping in a park in the west end, but after interviewing him, decided not to lay any charges.

There were stories about the Bottle Man that might help explain how he got to be the way he was, but we never knew if they were true.

Frampton said that the Bottle Man used to work as a window washer downtown and that one cold fall day he fell off a scaffold three stories up, landing on his feet. Apparently his boss tried to get him to go to the hospital but the Bottle Man wouldn't go. He said he felt fine and at the end of the day took the streetcar home. By the time he got to the neighbourhood, though, his back was hurting so bad he had to crawl all the way up the street. Frampton said it was a sight he'll never forget.

Ralph's mom knew the Bottle Man years ago and she remembered how he had been offered a chance to buy into a small chain of beauty salons in the west end. At the last minute, a guy who had been a good buddy for many years apparently jockeyed the Bottle Man out of the deal. Ralph's mom said the Bottle Man took that real hard and he'd been drifting ever since.

My old man told us the Bottle Man had three older brothers who would take turns beating the shit out of him. He said the Bottle Man just got hit about the head too much and went a little funny. That's why he tells us kids not to be so hard on the Bottle Man. Coming from my old man, that's something.

Whatever it was, the Bottle Man was different.

He lived alone in a small, dark basement apartment in the only duplex on our street. It was kind of run-down, not like the new ones they put up years later just down from my house, with their fake shutters and plastic planters. They were palaces by comparison.

Once, Tuck and I sneaked up real close to his only ground-level window and peeked in. All we could see were bottles – bottles on the couch, bottles on the faded living room chairs, bottles on the flimsy carpet, bottles on the coffee table, bottles on the bookshelves, bottles on the end tables. Beer, wine, whiskey, gin, pop, every variety. All of them were empty. It was no wonder he ended up with all those cuts and bruises on his face and hands. He probably fell over those damn bottles every time he went to watch the Leafs on television.

Tuck thought it was funny as hell. I don't remember laughing. At the time I remember just being a bit sad. It seems like the Bottle Man was a lonely stench of a character who had found some bizarre way of filling his tragic emptiness by cramming his tiny apartment with glass. No one ever explained it to me. It was just the kind of thing I put together myself over the years. If you believed half the stories they told about him, he couldn't have been feeling happy about his life. Maybe the bumps on the head, the bad business deal, the fall off the scaffold helped create the Bottle Man. Or maybe he just gave up on normal neighbourhood life and took to collecting bottles. I never really knew the answer.

You have probably figured out that, despite everything, I had a bit of a soft spot for the Bottle Man. It's not that he wasn't a pain in the ass. He was. Tuck was right too. He was crazy and maybe even dangerous. But the Bottle Man was like most people, he wasn't all bad.

I knew that for sure.

One late fall night when the smelt were running, I was down at the Kip Avenue pier on Lake Ontario watching the immigrant families pulling in their nets of slippery little fish and tossing them into pails of water. My mom used to tell us they were dirty and that she didn't want to see the things in our house, not even on Friday when eating fish was mandatory.

But I used to love watching those webbed nets appear out of the dark lake teeming with life, and watching our new neighbours' faces light up with excitement with their catch.

That night I got a little bit too excited. Backing up to make room for another full net of smelt, I fell back into the frigid lake. I was lucky I didn't hit my head on the concrete pier. But unfortunately, I wasn't much of a swimmer and I took in more water than Marilyn Bell did during her whole swim across Lake Ontario.

Apparently the three immigrant fishermen pulled me from the water but couldn't get me breathing. They struggled for a long minute before a smelly, dishevelled character pushed them away and started blowing into my lungs.

It was the Bottle Man, or so I learned later.

By the time the ambulance came, the Bottle Man was nowhere to be seen. He'd disappeared again.

When I got out of hospital I kept an eye out for the Bottle Man. I wasn't exactly sure what I would say but I sure wanted to thank him. Hell, the guy saved my life. I didn't see him for the longest time, and then one day I was swigging Orange Crush at Thorpe's Variety Store on Queen Street and I saw him through the big front window that looked across at our street.

'Got to run, Bill,' I said, placing my empty on the counter. 'See you later.'

The Bottle Man was halfway down Kip Avenue by the time I caught up with him. It must have been the new running shoes (black with yellow circles on them) that gave him that extra burst of speed. His grocery cart sounded like a glass symphony – all different sizes and shapes tumbling into one another. I thought they were going to burst into smithereens any moment.

The Bottle Man had a little bit of the devil in his eyes that day.

'Oh, it's you,' he said. 'I thought you were dead. Keep the hell out of the way or I'll ram you the way I did your friend Johnny Bower, the goalkeeper.'

The Bottle Man was enjoying this for some strange reason – a lot.

Meanwhile, I was halfway through the longest conversation I would ever have with this half-crazed creature with a passion for glass, who it just so happened had also saved my life a couple of weeks before.

'I just, wanted to say ... um ... thanks,' I managed to splutter.

He kept looking straight ahead, even though I was walking right beside him at this point.

'I guess you said it, then. Now get out of my way. I got to get to the beach, lots of bottles.'

That was the first time I had ever heard him talk about his habit, collecting the bottles, that is. For a moment I felt a little guilty for the nickname, the Bottle Man. It was Carruthers' idea, even though we all called him that now. Before I knew it, the next sentence was out of my mouth.

'How come you do it, collect all those bottles? How come—'

'Mind your own business, boy,' he spat back, his wheezing sounding like a pipe that was about to burst. 'Mind your business. Everybody has something they do. This is what I do. Mind your bloody business and get the hell away from me.'

He disappeared into the park.

I just stood there gaping.

I'm not sure I ever talked to the Bottle Man again.

I saw him around a lot – at the 48th Highlanders concert down at Kew Gardens, gaping at Christine, the cashier at the IGA grocery store before she went off to university, counting his change outside the Goof (Good Food) Restaurant to see if he had enough to go in for a coffee. But it wasn't the same. He seemed quieter. He wasn't yelling at anybody. It was like he had had all the old spirit sucked out of him. I kind of missed the old days when the Bottle Man was creating havoc every second day. Tuck said I was nuts.

We got the news that the Bottle Man had died one snowy Saturday morning just as the ball hockey game was about to start. Frampton came out and told my dad. He said that the Bottle Man had actually died a few days ago but nobody knew. Apparently he fell on some bottles at his apartment and couldn't get up. They figured he bled to death. All alone. The smell was so bad that the people next door finally called the cops. Maitland came and the neighbours said he kicked all the bottles out of his way, partly to clear a path, partly because he was so damned sad at what he saw. He was a religious man just like his dad.

I got to thinking how it was just like when Jimmy C died and how that was the first time I had ever seen the Bottle Man. Somehow I figured they were connected but I couldn't quite explain it. I missed them both, Jimmy C and the Bottle Man. Tuck couldn't quite figure out why. He said Jimmy C was a loser, and the Bottle Man, just crazy.

I didn't know. I just guessed they were people like the rest of us.

I wish I could tell you I went to the service at the funeral home down on Queen Street. But I didn't go. I actually started off in that direction and then chickened out. Nobody went, and I guess that makes sense. We never really got close to the Bottle Man.

You probably figured out where I went instead. I walked down to the pier at the foot of Kip Avenue and just stood looking out at the waves and the gulls. I didn't cry or anything, but I felt real sad. I couldn't understand exactly why. Maybe it was because I never really got to know the Bottle Man. Maybe it was because it seemed like such a waste, his life coming down to a stinking basement apartment full of bottles. It was more than I could figure out.

All I know was I couldn't get his words out of my head, the words he wheezed out when Jimmy C got run over by the East End Market truck.

'Jesus, I knew that guy.'

Love Match

God, she can hit the ball now, he thinks, as the yellow tennis ball bounces off her racquet and streaks towards his half of the green asphalt court.

'Fifteen love,' she says, louder than he thought necessary.

Focus, he says to himself.

Another tennis ball comes whirling towards him.

'Thirty love,' she says, louder still but with less of an edge.

Oh God, he stammers under his breath. Get in the game or it will be over.

And one more yellow blur bounces by him, waist high.

'Shit.'

'Pardon?'

'You heard me.'

And then another ball he can't get to.

'That's game then, one love for me.'

'Give me the ball.'

*

They'd been doing this for years now, ever since Hazel Morrison left in the heat of that July no one could forget a decade ago – left them both, slamming the back screen door for the last time, leaving only the reverberation of aluminium hitting an ill-fitted wood frame and the same bloody persistent fly trying to get in.

Soon after, he plucked the two old racquets from the wall of the garage like they were ripe peaches, too long on the tree, and handed one to Jody.

'Here, take this,' he said. 'We're going to learn tennis.'

He's not sure why he did that. He had played as a kid on the

Holy Cross Church courts; even competed for the Catholic Youth Organization or CYO, as they called it; he wasn't that good, didn't have the killer instinct on the courts, but he loved the game: the feel of the ball on the sweet spot of the racquet; hustling for the drop balls; smashing the passing shots that made your opponent look like he was standing still. He even grew to like wearing the whites, crisp and clean at the beginning of the game, soaked through at the end. He didn't give up tennis right away as a teenager. All the pretty girls from the convent school played and he liked to watch them bounce delicately across the court; it was a chance to get close to them by sharing the sweat-sprinkled courts and the icy pops afterwards.

Besides, it kept him from going home to the chaos of his falling-down family; Dad passed out on the couch, clutching a rum bottle like it was a teddy bear; Mom primly sipping diet Coke laced with rye on the shaded front porch; chipped dishes strewn across the kitchen; and garbage scattered around the backyard like a hurricane had hit.

'Where the hell have you been?' his father would slur as he tried to sit up, checking the bottle for one last hit.

'Tennis,' he'd mumble towards his bedroom.

Mom would step between them if she could, hushing them both before fists flew. Sometimes it didn't work.

Once, Sandy's father broke down the door of his room in a drunken midnight rage, accusing him of stealing his car. The police had impounded it the night before when he was caught going the wrong way on the highway. Sandy shoved him towards the doorway.

'Get the hell out of here, you drunken bastard,' he yelled. His father charged him, smashing a lamp, pushing Sandy into a corner. His mother could hear the ribs crack from the other room. By the time she got there, Sandy was whimpering in a corner, his great bear of a father passed out beside the desk he had collided with.

Tennis helped get him away from this 1960s Canadian picture-perfect postcard, at least for a while. Soon he started staying away from the courts. The formality, rules and straight lines became too rigid as he began to protest the world he'd been left by a generation of players who prided themselves on always keeping the ball inside the court – at least in public.

*

'That's out. It's your serve, Dad. Are you sure you're okay to play?'

'Yeah, why?'

'Maybe you're not into it right now.'

The nerve of her, he thinks. What does she mean am *I* okay? Who does she think *she* is? Am I really sweating this much, he wonders, looking up at the haze-hidden sun.

'I'm fine,' he says, repeating the mantra of his youth. 'What's the score?'

'Two games to love for the good-looking one.'

They laugh.

*

The day her mother left, Jody got up in the middle of the big separation speech and went downstairs to finish her laundry, like she had just been told her mother and father had traded in their Ford for a Chevy. Then she went to her room for the next month, emerging in her baggy pyjamas and her greasy brown hair only for the occasional piece of dry toast and pulpy orange juice.

Finally, her father took her reluctant hand to the public tennis courts around the corner, not as fancy as Holy Cross, but they would do. As the tall man and slouching daughter entered the gate of the Highland Courts, her father pointed his gnarled finger towards her and spoke as clearly as he could.

'Remember this, you and I need lots of love and there's no more love anywhere in the world than there is on a tennis court.'

She just looked up at her misty-eyed father like he was from another place and time and silently mouthed something he understood perfectly clearly. 'I hate your fucking guts.'

Somehow the tennis persisted. Not that Jody took to it right away. At first, she had trouble hitting the ball, then hitting it straight, then keeping it in the court. But this family ritual wasn't really about aces or overhead slams. It was to keep the ball moving back and forth, rallying so the other could receive it; keeping the conversation going.

Sandy Morgan knew nothing of textbook psychology but his instincts told him that was important. On a good day, it went something like this:

Swoosh.

'How's school going?'

Hustle.

Swat.

'Fine.'

Slice.

'Did you finish the project on Niagara Falls?'

Slam.

'Yes.'

Whack.

'Dad, can we just play tennis?'

Stop.

Lob.

'Okay.'

But there were other kinds of days that scared the life out of both of them. When she was 13, Jody locked herself in the bathroom of their modest wartime house for six straight hours, refusing to come out, refusing to speak, refusing to give up the only decent toilet in the house. Sandy thought he knew what was happening. He and Hazel had discussed how to handle this new stage on the telephone just a week ago. Exasperated, he huddled next to the bathroom door.

'Are you okay?'

'Fuck off, Dad. Really, fuck off.'

'Look, your mom and I have been talking about this.'

'You and Mom have been talking? About my fucking life? Both of you should fuck off. It's none of your fucking business.'

'Look, Jody, I don't appreciate your language and I need you to come out of the bathroom and talk about this. Right now.'

'Well, I need you to go away and leave me alone.'

'Jody.'

'I mean it.'

Sandy threw on his windbreaker and crossed the street to the Taylor house. Fred Taylor, a hockey buddy, who had a relaxed way of problem solving about him, was headed out for a beer and invited Sandy to come along for his usual ginger ale. He asked his stylish wife, Lorraine, if she'd check in on Jody in a couple of minutes. The two men commiserated about the Leafs and the Jays, Fred trying to keep Sandy distracted, even if only for a few minutes.

The truce seemed to work. Somehow Lorraine got Jody out of the bathroom and they called her mom on the phone.

When he got home from the pub, Sandy could hear strains of Bob Marley coming from Jody's bedroom. He kept his distance. He put on the television, hoping to catch the news on the CBC, hear some familiar voices, but he was holding his breath, wondering what would come next. Jody, now showered and in clean pyjamas, was closeted in her room, hoping she didn't have to talk to her dad again for a very long time.

Of course there would be other horrible patches, her unexplained temper tantrums, his silent brooding, the mysterious moments when she seemed unreachable; he too exasperated to know how to reach out. And there was always the question of the marriage ending. Did she blame him? Was she scarred for life? Or dealing with the reality of it in her own slow way? He didn't know and the uncertainty continued to gnaw at him like a rat chewing an electric cord as he lay in his sleepless bed, waiting for the jolt to hit him.

Two weeks later they were on the courts. They didn't talk so much the first time out after the incident, but they were playing, hitting the ball back and forth in a familiar family rhythm. Maybe this was their special time, their special place.

*

'God, your serve sucks today.'

'No kidding.'

'I can't throw the ball up straight into the air. Maybe it's the wind.'

'It's not the wind. And I don't mean what's the matter with your serve, as if you didn't know.'

He doesn't bite.

'What's the score?'

'Three love. Time you got going.'

'Okay, time for a comeback.'

'This I've got to see.'

*

Sandy Morrison thinks his wife actually began leaving the family years before that sweltering July. A friend started dragging his wife to lectures at the university and eventually Hazel applied to get accepted as a mature student. Sandy never put up an open fight but there was a kind of silent passive resistance. He had gone right from Grade 13 into the family aluminium siding business, which he now ran. The company did well and no one would deny that Sandy was successful. So he never said 'no' when he and Hazel talked about it, but his enthusiasm for the venture could only be measured by the thimble-full.

University changed his wife. Hazel's coiffed blonde hair became straggly, her beautiful peachy complexion gained lines that looked like question marks as she started pondering the meaning of her life and the world around her. Her soft edge got a little rough as she read politics, history and theology. She was becoming a different woman right before Sandy's rigid jaw and lost blue eyes. She studied psychology and eventually social work because she wanted to help the kind of kids she saw on the fringes of their changing neighbourhood.

There were changes in the Morrison household too. The dishes piled up in the kitchen and laundry had to wait a week or so now and Sandy had to drive Jody just about everywhere. He was working longer hours now. The economy was 'in the dumpster', as the guys at the pub would say. Sandy had to lay off his labourer, the one who actually did most of the onsite work. Now, Sandy had to work the office and do some labour. It was getting to be too much.

Many times Hazel tried to assure Sandy that it wasn't him that was the problem. It was about her. There was a quiet confrontation one night in the kitchen. She turned her soft green eyes toward him while her hands continued to labour amid the soapy suds in the sink and spoke softly yet firmly. 'It's not another man. You need to know that. I've just become another person. I have some new ideas I need to try out, different directions I want to go. And I have to do it alone. Can't you see?'

He didn't say much that day, but silently laid the blame on the university and its big ideas, for taking her away. He loved her too much to put it on her and couldn't see what he might have done differently.

'I don't know,' he moaned. 'I just don't get it.'

He began sleeping on the couch in the basement, his slender six-foot frame spilling onto the scarred coffee table they had sought out at a garage sale in the early, free and easy days of the marriage. He was steeling himself for her leaving.

When it came, it was too much to bear. There were months of bargaining and pleading and screaming.

'You're destroying a family,' he shouted one night while she was trying to get through a thick psychology text. 'You're ruining a little girl's life.'

'That's not true and you know it,' she cried, getting up from the kitchen table to grab a tissue for her nose. 'That's unfair. I'll be blocks away and Jody will be fine.' She threw the tissue box back on to the counter.

Later that night in a quieter moment, he came and put his head on her stomach as she read on the couch.

'Look, you quit school and I'll hire a new man and we can get back to normal.'

But it didn't work.

The day she moved out, he took the set of matching grey suitcases she was packing and tossed them into the backyard.

'There, why don't you pack them outside, it's a beautiful bloody day,' he shouted at the top of his lungs.

Hazel, her stringy hair still wet from a quick shower, ran to retrieve them and he started tossing her clothes all over the yard. They smacked into each other in the kitchen a few minutes later and they were both shaking so hard they couldn't speak. He came towards her with a rage in his eyes she had never seen and his hand upraised ever so slightly. She held her hands up to protect herself. He fell to his knees.

'Until death, do us part – do you remember that? Don't say another word about finding yourself. Just fucking go. Go.'

She did.

*

'That's four love. Dad. Do you want to call it quits?'

There she goes playing mother again. Is she worried I'm going to have a heart attack here on the court or that I'm having some kind of breakdown. She's been talking about psychology too much with her mother.

'You know I never quit.'

'I know.'

‘Whose serve is it?’

Jody just shakes her head. It looks like they’re going to finish after all.

*

Sandy’s dad lost his licence for good after several more drunk-driving incidents. He took a cab to work every day and tried to manage the company, but more often than not he went to lunch and never came back. Eventually he would disappear for days on end, the family waiting for the phone call from the hospital, the detox, the police or whoever calls when a drinker finally succumbs in the downward spiral of death.

The call came one wintry morning when Sandy was jumping into his shiny grey suit for a friend’s father’s funeral.

‘Your dad is dead,’ the telephone told him. Sandy kept hearing the words over and over as he drove to his father’s bachelor apartment. He had taken the apartment six months earlier. Sandy’s mom had quit drinking and kicked him out of the house. Somehow she knew where this was headed. The police stopped him at the door of the apartment.

‘You are not going in there, young man,’ said the big constable, blocking his path. Even from the doorway, the stench of blood and putrid decomposing flesh hit Sandy like a blast from a furnace from some corner of some hell. His father had been in there for days before a neighbour called the police. Fell. Bumped his head. Bled to death. Sandy hit the street, spewing vomit all over a garbage can lying on its side between apartment buildings while a clutch of hatless firefighters sipped coffee.

Within a year, Sandy, his mom and the lead labourer were running the business, trying desperately to breathe new life into a failing enterprise.

*

‘I think you’re losing your game, Dad. Maybe you should be hanging up that racquet,’ Jody yells across the net.

Sandy grimaces. He has no response.

'That's five love. Last chance, old man.'

He could sense her trying to cheer him up, get him back on track. He takes a deep breath. He can return that verbal volley at least.

'Careful, you're not so young yourself any more. Get ready for my best serve.'

'I'm scared shitless.'

*

At first Sandy wished he and Hazel had had a boy as well as a girl. He was an only child himself and he knew how self-centred you could get, although he would never say it like that. His mom could not possibly get pregnant again – doctor's orders. It gave her a chance to defy Mother Church with birth control. She loved that. Hazel just didn't want any more kids, simple as that. She had replaced herself and now there was no more need for any children. Sandy was bitter at first, but he didn't say too much, preferring to dote on his one and only.

Right from the beginning you could see Jody would be tall, like her mother. She let her brown hair grow long over the years, though she always tied it back when she played tennis. Awkward on the courts the first few years, her tennis grew with her. She had long slender legs that helped her bound across the courts like a majestic deer. She grew to become a good tennis player, smart too.

Sandy marvelled at how the boys just suddenly started hanging around one day and then were always there. Jody would be studying at the kitchen table with Stewart one week, camping with Frank the next, going to the movies with Tyler, then a few more serious dates with Jamie and Hans. David was different. For a year they were stuck to each other like glue. Jody was wearing more makeup, displaying her midriff, flirting with David at every opportunity. They went to her

Grade 12 prom together and then spent a week together at a cottage on Lake Simcoe. Hazel approved; Sandy just shrugged.

But later that summer, they broke up. The makeup disappeared and David disappeared. Poof. Gone.

'So, did you break up with him or what?' Sandy asked one day over popcorn and a bad Hollywood movie on the VCR.

'Typical dad question.'

'Meaning?'

'Dumb.'

'Thank you.'

'We were bored.'

'It didn't seem like it.'

'Trust me.'

'Did you talk to him on the phone or face to face?'

'Dad question.'

'Okay, help me out.'

'Email,' she said with her wonderful sarcastic bite.

'Oh, are you okay?'

'Yes.'

'Is he? Okay, I mean?'

David was a shaggy-dog kind of fellow nobody could have disliked. Sandy kind of missed him.

'I don't know. Press Start, would you?'

Jody did really well all through school. Straight A's in Grade School, B-pluses in high school, with all its hormonal distractions, up to her last year, when she really bore down, swore off the boys, for a while, anyways, and spent hours writing and researching and acing all her subjects. There was no question she would go to university. Her mom insisted. Her dad just nodded in silent acquiescence.

The moment he found out Jody had been accepted at the university she really wanted to go to, Sandy was speechless, then furious. It was the University of Prague – yeah, that Prague, the one in Europe. What the hell! He took his tennis racquet out behind the garage and started whacking old balls onto the railway line as hard as he had ever hit anything before in his life. The way he had wanted to hit his old man. Whack! Whack! Whack! Whack! Whack! Thirty minutes later, he came back into the house with perspiration dripping down his face and great gobs of tears in his eyes and yelled at Jody. 'You're going to Czechoslovakia? Why the hell are you doing that? Why do you need to go so far away?'

There was a long pause before Jody spoke. The hum of the fridge filled the gap.

'Uh, Dad, it's the Czech Republic now. Remember, the separation from Slovakia.'

Fuck.

She was being a smart ass, trying to get him off track. All he could think was, another goddamned separation. Nothing good is going to come of this.

That's when she said it. 'Dad, come on, we're going to learn tennis now.'

Out they went to the courts, one more time.

*

The ball comes straight at him, hitting him in the middle. He had no time to react. God, he gasps.

'That's it. I win. Six love. That's game, set and match. Guess the old teacher is taking lessons from the pupil now, eh, Dad,' she crows, leaping over the net.

He can't respond. He just chokes out some kind of strange sound, uttering under his breath. 'Cheek.'

They sit on the usual park bench under the shade of the maple and watch the kids on the middle court bang the ball all over the place. Those were the days, he thinks.

Jody wants to talk.

'Dad, I'm not going away to get away from you. I'm not leaving you. I'm just moving on, beginning my own life in a very exciting place. I'm studying European History. It's one of the top schools for that. I got a scholarship. But believe me, I'll miss you.'

Her words and tone of voice have a familiarity that takes his breath away.

'I just don't get it. Why do you have to go so far away?'

'Dad, remember how you taught me the best place to wait for the ball when playing tennis is the back of the court, just inside the line? How you said, you can wander all over to make returns, but you have to try and get back to that one spot that puts you in place for the next shot? Remember that?'

He looks at her but has trouble seeing her.

'You're my spot on the court, just inside the line. You're it. Dad, this isn't like Mom. I'll always come back to you, even if it's only to get ready for the next adventure. But I've got to travel around a bit, see what life is serving up. I can't afford to wait here and see what comes my way. I have to go after it. Sometimes you have to go to the net.'

She pauses, takes a breath.

'You taught me that too, you know.'

'I did?' he says, almost inaudibly, suddenly feeling ancient and no wiser, knowing damn well she had really learned it on her own.

The ball from the kids' game dribbles through the gate to the courts and ends up at their feet. Jody stands up and tosses it back.

'Those kids don't know what they're doing out there,' he says, as they start back towards the house.

'That's because their dad's not showing them how,' she says.

'I guess,' he whispers, struggling to see her cheeky smile through the mist in his eyes. 'I guess.'

Peter's Denial

Canon Peter slipped out of his Easter vestments and into the rain-soaked parking lot of Christ Anglican Church.

It had been another fine service. Just enough pomp to remind his parishioners that they were not so different from their Roman Catholic cousins worshipping across the street; just enough references to current political issues to keep them from crossing town to the trendy United Church.

But Canon Peter was distracted and didn't enjoy his apparent success. He needed to fly. He had ten minutes to cross town so he could spend the lunch hour with Lily. She had to leave sharply at one.

Canon Peter met Lily one of those wrenching days following Christmas two years ago. Even his most faithful parishioners seemed to have deserted him for the sunny climes of Florida and his traditional post-Yule depression set in. Met is probably not the right word. Canon Peter arranged a rendezvous with her through the escort ads in the left-leaning weekly. She was everything he had ever desired in a woman. Her skin was cool and shimmering against his fuzzy, pudgy fifty-year-old body. He revelled in the curve of her elegant breasts, the scent of her luxuriously long neck, the piercing green of her eyes. He fed on the lilt of her sing-song voice.

He told himself he was offering the salvation of an intelligent tryst, one that might help lift her from a life of sinful depravity.

But the times when he most enjoyed her soft touch and her moaning and slithering beneath him followed his sermons on the perils of the sexual revolution.

Or following a particularly holy season in the liturgical calendar.

Canon Peter could see Lily was home when he hurried up the steps of her mid-town townhouse. She was tall, much taller than Canon Peter; blonde, much blonder than he imagined possible. Lily had the kind of figure Canon Peter could have only dreamt of not so long ago. The way she decorated her shapely figure made her remarkably different from any woman the good Canon would find in his church, or his marriage bed.

Canon Peter was in a hurry to hold Lily in his hairy arms, be held in her unquestioning embrace; lost in her scent, found in her warmth. An hour earlier the pulpit had drained his soul. He longed for Lily's breath against him to fill him again with the spirit to continue.

Lily wanted to talk.

'I saw you today,' Lily said, dropping her eyes and looking slightly away from him, an affectation that normally drove him to distraction. This time, however, it was her words that unsettled him, sent a shock wave to his very soul.

'You what?' he gasped.

'I saw you.'

'Saw me, where?' he questioned, the strain in his voice revealing his growing anxiety.

'In that museum you call a church. Not only that, you saw me and made it clear that I didn't belong there.'

'What are you talking about? I didn't see you ...'

'You may not have recognized me, but you definitely saw me. And you managed to stare right through me and focus on the mink coat behind me.'

Lily pulled her outrageous pink felt hat out of the cupboard in the hall. She waved it at the good Canon, reliving her masquerade in the snake-like queue that had shaken his sweaty palms before it slowly spit the faithful from the holy edifice into the late morning sunlight.

Canon Peter turned pale.

'I don't remember any of this,' he stated with exaggerated conviction.

'Don't remember or don't want to fess up?'

Canon Peter didn't respond.

To change the subject, he took the billfold from his wallet and placed it ever so precisely on the marble mantle.

Lily's sheets always offered the good Canon so very much: passion, warmth, compassion, play and fantasy that bordered on naughtiness. In her bed, he was transformed. He became both man and child, lover and loved, pastor and pastored to. He was alive. The frantic pace of his breathing, the pitch of his moaning reminded him of the life within that longed to be free. For a long moment the good Canon forgot the conversation in the living room. He lay placidly in Lily's sweet bed.

Yet he couldn't quite shake this post-coital nagging. There was something about this intimacy with Lily that was perhaps illusory; or better still, real, but somehow too obsessive. It wasn't just that he felt like a money changer in the temple, it was something more, something even more consuming than the mercantile act.

And yet . . .

Canon Peter gazed upon his lovely Lily. He had pulled the sheet over his midriff. She lay flat on her stomach with her breasts pressed against the sheet, looking like half-moons, her beautifully tight bottom taunting him with naked arrogance. The good Canon couldn't take his eyes off of her.

Lily looked away.

She wanted to talk again.

'They don't touch.'

'I beg your pardon?' he gasped.

'Your Christians, they don't touch each other.'

'What do you mean, they don't touch? They don't go to church to touch . . .'

'I know that. But have you ever watched them? They go out of their way not to touch. Even that "kiss of peace" thing, it's like a Puritan dance. They only touch each other accidentally with "excuse me's" dripping from their tight little lips.'

'You're being cruel.'

'Maybe. But I'm trying to give you a dose of reality here, good Canon.'

Canon Peter was startled. She never mentioned his title. This kind of comment about his church, his holy orders, had a way of bruising his soul. Canon Peter liked to steer clear of that kind of pain. That's what pushed him into theology in the first place. He needed a way of offering good news, not just for others but …

Lily interrupted his feeling sorry for himself.

'You just can't admit that they don't really love each other; they don't even know what it means. And they no more love the poor people who haven't any voices or franchises you preached about this morning than …'

'That's the *disenfranchised* …'

'Whatever. They can't even love each other. I heard them whispering about the guy at the back who stank of booze and God knows what else. It's like they're wearing their Sunday best too tight and they've got their eyes so fixed on those old hymn books, they can't see who's sitting right next to them.'

'That's just not true. And anyways, who does know how to love so perfectly? You? Your friends?'

'Maybe we could teach you all something about loving. At least we could show you how to hold each other like people are meant to be held. Are you forgetting what you were like when you first came to me?'

Canon Peter ignored the remark, though he remembered full well.

Lily continued.

'You church people should stop thinking about your

righteous souls so much and pay attention to your uptight bodies. That's where people are at. And, by the way, I think me and my friends really do know something about loving. We give people what they want, a little tender loving care, you know. We tell them they're alright, they're beautiful, they're good to be with. When was the last time you preached a sermon on that sort of thing?'

Lily lifted her long curved body from her sheets, offering Canon Peter a long, leisurely look at her gifts. She then slipped into the bathroom.

Canon Peter mumbled something unintelligible under his breath. He began putting on his clothes. The lovemaking, the conversation, had left him feeling out of sorts. He needed to regain his composure. He straightened the sheets, put on his clothes: socks, underwear, shirt, collar, slacks, shoes, jacket, crucifix.

As he sat on Lily's best living room chair, sipping a dry white wine, he let himself slip into a kind of altered state. He fought the usual dream for some time but eventually relented as he always did. It began to fill his weary head the way Lily filled the hole in his soul.

A grim, grey hawk of a man dominates his dream. His bony face always scares Canon Peter. The grey hawk-man carries a young boy towards an inviting sea. There is a moment of panic or struggle. He can never quite tell what is happening at this point though he has dreamed it a thousand times. The boy falls or is pushed into the sea. The man stares out into the sea as if frozen. Then the man turns from the sea, calmly, ignoring the boy's cries for help. The boy appears to drown in the sea. Canon Peter thinks he can see a smile, or a sneer, cross the grey hawk-man's otherwise rigid face.

Lily burst through the bathroom door, painted, primped and pampered. She has to be off to work at a cross-town hotel, where there was a convention of psychiatrists gathering. Business would be good. She had several appointments. Canon Peter's other dream was about to end.

Still, she wanted to finish the conversation. Canon Peter wished it had ended.

'You don't believe it, do you?' she asked, while stuffing her belongings into the black leather purse the good Canon gave her for Christmas last year in a careless moment of abandon.

'Don't believe what?' he responded flatly. The good Canon was tiring of the fight. This was not why he fled the church parking lot in such haste this morning.

'Any of it.'

'Any of what?'

'Any of the stuff you preach. You know. Jesus turning into mighty Hercules, shoving the rock from his tomb. Those miracles. Mary having a baby and still being a virgin. Right. And Jesus walking on top of some lake. That we're supposed to love people who hate us. Jesus wiping away all the bad stuff we do because he died on a cross. Poor people being special. That liberal stuff you were talking about this morning ...'

'That's *liberation theology* ...'

'Whatever. You still don't believe it. The only thing I can remember from Sunday School ...'

He gasped. 'You went to Sunday School?'

Lily normally talked about herself even less than the good Canon. This, she would cut short. 'Of course. You think I spring from the womb a full-grown escort? I was a good Baptist until the youth pastor tried to get his hands on what you spend the better part of your allowance on.'

'Jesus.'

'Exactly. But at least they tried to teach me that your Jesus is all about love and that's the most important thing in the Bible, right?'

'Well . . .'

'See, you don't really believe it. How come nobody went near that old drunk at the back of the church this morning? How come they whispered about him on the way out after the service? Your Christians are good at talking about love but they never *do* anything about it.'

'That's not true and you know it. The churches have been at the forefront of every great social movement of this century . . .'

Canon Peter wanted to put an end to this. He began to dig into his seminary church history mental files, his speciality.

'You mean you're socialists?'

'God, no. I'm talking about social movements, you know the statements we make about native rights, the poor, the homeless . . .'

'Talk is cheap. That's why I never went back to the damn church.'

Canon Peter still wanted to turn the tables though he feared it was too late. 'How come you picked today to return to the fold?' His voice dripped with sarcasm.

'I wanted to see how you performed with your clothes on for a change.' Lily laughed bitterly.

Canon Peter smiled weakly.

'I do believe, you know.' He spoke flatly, deliberately, something he did unknowingly when in a tight corner. 'And so do my parishioners. Sure, we don't love with great abandon the way we should. We're not on the cutting edge like Oscar Romero or Desmond Tutu or even some of the downtown churches. Hell, we're Canadians, Anglicans. We're cautious about everything. I agree, we have lots to learn. But don't start telling me we don't believe. That's just bullshit.'

'Canon Peter,' Lily mocked.

'Get over it.'

'I still say, if you don't know how to love the guy next to you, if you don't know how to even reach out to the lady next to you, you'll never know how to love bad people or the stinking drunks at the back of the church.'

Canon Peter was on his feet and at the door. This was getting too close to the bone. 'I think that is just about enough. You have no right to talk to me like this. I won't be abused—'

He stopped abruptly.

The good Canon made his way down the stairs and into the cobblestoned street. Lily followed a moment later, speeding out of her driveway past him in her red sports car.

He sat in his car a very long time, gripping the wheel, shaking and weeping more tears than he could ever remember shedding. Finally, he looked up into his rear-view mirror. He thought for a moment he could see the grey hawk-man staring back at him. He drove away.

The next few days were a blur for Peter. He went neither to his church nor to his home. He slept in his car and drove around all day, stopping in greasy spoons for late-night coffees and stale doughnuts. It was as if he was on a life and death mission but didn't know where it began or ended. The grey hawk-man haunted him and he avoided looking in the mirror.

Finally, he cleaned himself up and went home. The next day he went to see his bishop, an ageing, balding man with whom he had never really gotten on. The older man listened while Peter spoke for a long time, wiping his eyes intermittently. There was a pregnant pause.

Then the bishop spoke simply. 'I think you are right, Peter. You have lost your faith.'

Peter found himself unable to speak. All he could do now was stare at his feet.

A month later a parcel arrived at Lily's townhouse.

She opened it and read the attached note.

I have left the church. And my family. I am living at the lake for a while and hope to find myself, get things sorted out.

Thanks for saving my life. Peter.

P.S. The book is for you. You understand it better than I ever did.'

Lily thumbed through the pages of Peter's leather-bound Bible.

Out on the street a group of young men fresh from the pub a block away heard the sound of a woman singing at the top of her voice.

'Jesus loves me, this I know, for the Bible tells me so ...'

Paradise

Georgie sweeps the undergrowth of brown, black and grey snips from the floor of the shop at the suburban mall. It is called 'The Barber Shop' but ought to be 'Georgie's'.

*

After years of cutting, trimming and styling, Georgie thought he had a deal to buy the business from the owner, who also runs the women's salon in the same newly renovated mall. But once he gathered the money together, the big Greek owner dismissed him with a wave of his hairy hand.

'Sorry, no deal,' he said.

*

Georgie locks the shop door and hurries for the bus that takes him twenty blocks to his second-floor apartment in the brown three-storey walk-up on the edge of the city. Georgie sits in his customary spot at the back of the bus. He closes his eyes and runs his fingers through his slick black hair. For a barber, his hair is oddly cut. It is neatly shaped but off base, tilted like a toupee that doesn't quite fit. He is tall for a man from his native country, with strong legs, remnants from his days on the football pitch. They stretch out beneath the seat in front. His dark eyes close and his mind drifts. Georgie is tired after ten hours of cutting hair, trimming beards, cleaning up. Another day working for the big Greek, he thinks. Twenty heads of hair, cut. Another day closer to Natalie. Now, he is looking forward to the serenity of his simple apartment.

*

The few friends who have been inside Georgie's one-bedroom apartment are the only ones with a sense of the real man. He came here after the divorce. At first, he hated it, refused to come directly home after work. He spent hours in the dark English pub around the corner, lingering over the greasy fish and chips and sipping red draught beer before slinking to his bare walls and his single bed. Over time, that changed. As he slowly bought furniture and especially books, it became something else. It was home, but much more. In a kind of ironic bliss, the apartment became both refuge and escape; mistress and family; home and vacation.

Sometimes he would come home and sit silently in the dark, retracing the steps of his day, like watching silent black-and-white movies on the ceiling; sometimes he would come in and turn on every light, the small-screened television and the brand new radio and imagine being surrounded by raucous friends. Over time, it had become a place of warmth and comfort he welcomed.

Mostly it was because of his books.

*

The grey steel door opens to a literary sanctuary. Every wall is covered with books, even in the kitchen and bathroom. There are piles of paperbacks on the coffee table, books in a basket near the fake fireplace and stacks of pristine new releases in hardback on the bedside table. At one end of his purple floral pull-out couch, where Natalie sometimes sleeps, though it's been a while, there are three books he is considering reading next: a giant tome on Canada's Mennonites; a new writer's attempt to get inside the head of a young girl scarred for life by the atomic blast over Hiroshima; and lighter fare set in the midst of the Stratford Shakespearean Festival.

*

Sometimes when Georgie is in his friends' homes, he escapes the soft-core gossip and hockey talk and wanders through the house looking for the books that line their shelves or lie unread by their bedside tables. He learns a lot about his friends that way. If friends tried to figure out Georgie by the books in his apartment, they wouldn't be able to discern any clear pattern. But they would get the scent of his obsession. He remembers Robertson Davies writing in one of his thick novels of a man who was obsessed with books and good literature and the feeling of joy and superiority he gained from surrounding himself with these volumes – even though he never read them. Georgie reads his books.

He used to have a mug that sat on his favourite living room book case. It was stamped with a quote about how books offered a taste of heaven to their readers. He'd bought it at a church bazaar one crisp fall morning years ago for just fifty cents. When he was part of a happy couple, the mug had a place of honour in the kitchen and there were good-natured tussles for the mug at tea time. Once, in the heat of jostling for the mug, it fell between him and his wife, hit the kitchen linoleum and burst apart at the handle. They glued it back together and it was as good as new – almost. He lost the mug in the murk of a marriage gone sour a few years later.

When he is asked about his marriage, Georgie shrugs his shoulders or sticks his nose in a book until the topic evaporates. For some of his friends, that is enough. The separation and divorce sneaked up on him, he insists in his own internal conversation on the matter. But the signs were there. Creeping disinterest that invades like cancer; fading affection; absences, both real and imagined; anger without explanation. Her tension grew; he withdrew further. There were few explosions really, mostly a growing silence reminiscent of an insignificant death - that is if there is ever such a passing. Georgie tries not to think too much about it all now.

Instead, he immerses himself more and more in his books, all the heavy weights of Canadian fiction: Margaret Laurence, Margaret Atwood and Matt Cohen. He cried when he heard how Matt had died of cancer after he had written about his brother falling victim to the same damned disease. He likes the so-called old guard and the new kids on the block too: Timothy Findley, Mordechai Richler, Alistair MacLeod, Robertson Davies, Barbara Gowdy, and Katherine Govier; he has a special place in his heart for the immigrant Canadians, Nino Ricci, Michael Ondaatje and Rohinton Mistry.

He may not be a flag-waving zealot but Georgie supports his adopted home by buying its best books. More importantly, they support him. They are both his window on his new home and his shelter from the harshest parts of his life – the low-paying work, the failed marriage, the business misadventure. When he was younger and unspoiled by life and love, he tried to scratch out poems about the importance of books. He squirms at his efforts today.

'As I sit surrounded by my books and dreams/ I think of you,' one said.

Another time, he wrote, 'All that matters now are the books that line these walls/ protecting me from the sensuous world outside.'

It started when he was ten years old after arriving in Canada from Portugal. Georgie attended Cardinal Newman Roman Catholic School in one of the rougher parts of the city, where the teachers looked stressed from the first bell in the morning but where they spent long hours in a special classroom marked 'ESL', teaching him how to read in English. He moved from picture books to stories about stinky lunchroom sandwiches, especially written to make boys like him from other countries feel at home. He devoured books the way Vincenzo, in the story, swallowed his smelly meat sandwiches.

Things might have been different had his father not died when he was sixteen, a year behind in high school but showing great potential, particularly in English, his adopted tongue. He might have been a teacher or a writer. The call from the foreman at the factory came in the middle of the night and Georgie took the phone from his trembling mother, who couldn't make out what the gruff Scot was saying but knew instinctively that it was bad news.

'He's dead,' Georgie said, dropping the phone and collapsing into his mother's frail frame. The *Spectator* ran a four-paragraph story on the accident, saying there would be no inquest and listing the deceased as a Mr George Borges, which wasn't quite accurate.

Georgie picked up a job cleaning tables in the food court at the mall and began hanging around the barber shop, talking to the Greek and playing cards with the customers while they waited for their trims. He took a course downtown all one winter and then walked into the shop, his naturally tanned face beaming widely as a trembling hand held up his freshly minted 'Barber's Certificate'. It was Friday afternoon so they gave him a chair and stuck his name to the fading mirror. He started cutting and he's been there ever since.

He liked cutting hair even though friends tried to get him to look for a better paying job a number of times over the years. Each head of hair was a challenge, but a limited one. Every haircut represented a commitment, a problem that could be solved in half an hour. There was a definite beginning and end to each enterprise. He was in charge. He could his express his creativity but without revealing too much, without risking all. Most of the customers were too involved in their mundane worries to complain about a missed part or a cut that revealed too much of their pedestrian looks. Without realizing it, Georgie had settled into a groove over the years. He liked his work. He was good with his hands as they snipped and buzzed suburban scalps. He had a keen eye for lining up sideburns, making bangs straight, making everything fit. He liked being a barber. He just wanted to own his own shop. Be his own man.

*

Georgie picks up the book he has chosen to take him into his literary altered state, the story of an affair and a murder in Stratford, and settles in under the covers. It has received some poor reviews but he is going to make up his own mind. He loves the scent and feel of a new book, inky and mysterious; it feels right in his hands, just the right heft. He opens the book for the first time, inhales the scent, and starts to read. Immediately he is immersed. He's lost in a world of someone else's making. The gravelly-voiced jazzman on the radio is introducing the latest compact disc from the sultry Vancouver Island singer and pianist. Could heaven be far off?

After a while, Georgie drifts off to sleep, his book still in his hands, Natalie in his dreams.

Sunday with Natalie finally comes. He takes her to the park and they play on the swings, taking turns pushing each other, laughing out loud at the silliness. They have lunch at a fast-food place near his apartment, then they head home to read some stories and take a nap. The picture Georgie keeps of Natalie at work is a year out of date. She seems so much older now, talks a blue streak, keeps her hair short and smart and is getting long-legged and athletic at ten. Just like her mother. He thinks of how physical Natalie's mom was when she was younger. Tall and a natural athlete, she played basketball from an early age and got into volleyball at university. They tried playing tennis when they were first married but he was too awkward, too slow, and they abandoned it over time, not really talking about why. Maybe we can talk now, he thinks. Perhaps enough time has passed and we can put our differences aside for Natalie's sake.

The sky is dark and threatening as he approaches the bungalow Natalie shares with her mother and the broker from the big firm downtown. He's very smart but somehow unable to smile. Georgie frowns at this thought.

Natalie's mother greets them at the door. 'Hi, darling. In you go for supper,' she says to Natalie. Georgie turns to leave but is stopped by the rare sound of his name coming from his former wife's stern pursed lips. 'Georgie, I want to talk to you.'

He responds, 'Good, so do I. I mean . . .'

She laughs.

He is suddenly aware just how much he misses that sound. Subtle, not horsey the way the young girls at the mall snort as they wander past the shop.

'I think it's time we got civil with each other, for Natalie's sake, you understand. I want you to come more often; take her on the weekends, keep in touch about school, that sort of thing. I think it's time.'

He is taken aback.

'Yes,' he mutters. 'I would really like a more recent school photo too.'

Natalie's mother slips inside the house for a minute and reappears with a strip of headshots from school; it is the newer Natalie in her purple jumper, all sophisticated but with a spark of the old mischief in her dark eyes.

'I also found this,' she says, handing him a small cardboard gift box.

'Thanks,' he whispers.

'Thought you might want it,'

Then she disappears inside the house.

He doesn't open the package right away. He doesn't have to. He knows what's inside. He can tell from the size and shape of the box and the look on his former wife's face. She has done a good thing.

Georgie gets home and puts the kettle on. He is dying for a cup of tea. He is feeling strangely different now, not jubilant, but perhaps back on track, with a sense of purpose. He and Natalie will be seeing a lot more of each other. Things were going to be okay with her mother. They will talk about school and make plans for their daughter. That's the way it should be.

Natalie has suffered too much already. Sins of the father, as they say.

He makes the tea and lets it steep. He likes it strong.

I'm going to tell the Greek that I'll make him an offer, he thinks. If that doesn't work out, I'll walk; open my own place across the city; start fresh. We'll see.

For now, though, he still has his place, these comforts. He looks at the book-cluttered walls around him. They're like fat cushions insulating from the world, keeping him safe and warm, and yet opening up worlds of a different kind.

And now he has his tea mug again. It is different from what he remembers, older, changed, cracked, but somehow whole again. And he thinks of his new relationship with the woman who was his wife, and of his new life, which is perhaps just now starting.

He pours the steaming tea into the white mug. A black box is painted on it with words etched in red in the box. 'I have always imagined that paradise will be a kind of library.' – 'Jorge Luis Borges.'

He opens his book, puts the steaming tea to his lips.

Paradise.

Redemption

Andrew Stone's legs stiffened as he slowly climbed the twenty steps leading to the tiny room he shared with his wife. His cheeks were puffy red, his brow furrowed and the grey of his eyebrows pushed toward the crown of his head. He caught his breath. One foot followed the other and his knees cracked loudly. With his gnarled hand on the cracked railing, he steadied himself.

On the landing the old man stopped, mopped his forehead with a dusty handkerchief, caught his breath again and wiped his hands on the back of his trousers. Almost cursing, Stone turned to look behind and wondered if the landlord had added a step since morning. Perhaps it was time to find a ground-floor room. He was getting too old for this climbing and it might be good for June if she wanted to go out. But that would have to wait. He turned and went into the room.

The little grey man peeled off his jacket, tie and vest and hung them methodically in the clothes closet, shed his shoes in favour of his more comfortable slippers and shuffled to the bathroom. Stone studied his reflection in the mirror for some time then worked his face with his hands, hoping to deny the exhaustion. After washing his face and hands, he combed the few silver hairs that crossed his pointed head, frowned sternly at his image and trudged out to see his wife.

June Stone, crippled from polio for more than thirty years, was asleep in her chair by the window. It was from this vantage she liked to watch Andrew on his way to the food plant where he worked as a clerk.

She was proud of him as he moved in his stiff quick way

across the lane; and happy when she saw him return every evening at half-past five, the supper's meat tucked under his arm.

But she did not begrudge him the things she lacked – not the chance to get out of the room, nor the sense of pride that came with his work. No, and not even the willing feet which took him through the back lanes to work every day. She was proud of her husband of these past forty years, proud of the calm way he handled one disappointment after another, year after year. Stone always had some little encouragement for her, every day, though it seemed to get harder over the years.

'We'll get by, June,' he'd say when the factory cut everyone's hours or when wages were frozen yet again. 'As long as we've got each other, we'll get by.'

This determination allowed June to forget her sick body and let her drift into her dreams by the window, forgetting the pain.

That was often how Stone found his wife after his day at the factory. For a moment, he hesitated from awakening her. She looked peaceful, and pretty too, he thought, stoking back a strand of grey-black hair from her eyes. The eyes were closed now but when open were as green as the frozen limes which arrived daily at the factory. They were still the eyes that had drawn him to June and the ones that offered often silent understanding through the years. There was, of course, less sparkle since the sickness.

Stone drifted into the past without consent.

*

It was a sweetly warm summer thirty years ago that had robbed June Stone of her ability to walk. It came suddenly. For the first two days she had lain in her feverish bed. Then her feet became weak and useless. Within a week the virus had somehow crept to her waist, leaving her limbs paralysed.

Hundreds of people all over the country died of the disease

that year, including many children. June was thankful to be alive.

But Andrew was stricken with his own virus. A part of him died that summer too. His sickness was as real as his wife's yet impossible for any physician to diagnose. Stone was sick with a twisted sense of guilt. Before June's polio struck, she had been working an extra three nights a week at the Woolworth's department store to try and send Stone to his night-school classes. She had become tired and weak. He blamed himself for her illness. It didn't make sense, but no matter.

Two years later he felt the heavy weight of guilt again as he pawned June's wedding ring. It was the saddest moment of his life. The ring, he remembered, was beautiful, a bright gold band with rose-shaped diamonds. Andrew had been barely able to un-fist his hand to turn it over to the sweaty broker. It had been June's most treasured possession, her only piece of jewellery, in fact. But she had refused to let him give up the night-school classes that were so important to their future, even knowing she would never see the ring again. Times were tough and the two hundred dollars was needed.

However, just three months ago, Andrew had seen the chance for his redemption. His foreman had asked for one of the men to work two extra hours daily doing the plant sweeping while the regular cleaner was visiting relatives in Europe after a family funeral. Billy O'Neil, a bear of a man with pot belly and drooping moustache, just laughed the first time Stone told him he was interested.

'I was expecting one of those young bucks to come forward, what with their expensive cars and their girls and all, but you, Stoney, I'll have to think about that one,' he barked as he ushered Stone out of his sweltering little cubby hole of an office.

But no one else volunteered for the extra hours; it wasn't lucrative enough, and so after half a dozen conversations with

O'Neil, the brash sweaty sceptic finally gave in, but not without issuing a warning.

'Listen, old man,' he snarled without affection. 'If you can't do the work, tell me. I won't have this place looking like a pig pen when the health inspectors come around. It will mean my . . . and your job. You got that? Start on Monday.'

But Stone didn't need the caution. For the first time in years he had become excited about something and he felt a twinge of the old pride in his chest. He smiled broadly, thinking of how June would react to his ruse. He could almost see the sparkle return to her green eyes.

There was something else, though. In the past year June's health had been deteriorating quickly. The doctors said it was normal for a woman her age and with her polio. He was afraid he would lose her. All the while he also knew he could go first. He had always known deep down that was the way it would be. Living without June was something he refused to contemplate. None of this made him hesitate about taking the extra work. He knew what he wanted. His body would just have to keep up. Would keep up.

Still, he felt time was running out. With one week to go in his extended hours at the factory, Andrew felt weary, though buoyed by the knowledge that he would soon present June with the gift of a lifetime. He saw it as a chance to start over again.

*

June Stone shifted her head in the worn chair by the window and Stone was again conscious of her. The lines around her mouth moved ever so slightly as she spoke in her dream. She was pale, as those who spend all their time indoors are, yet her skin had always been remarkably beautiful and now she escaped the chalky look of the sick. June tried to turn on her side, bumped into the arm of the chair and awoke, slightly startled.

'Well, it's Andrew home then. I must have dropped off. Are you home late again? I've never seen you late so often in all these years.'

Andrew just smiled.

'Want some soup, June?' he asked, straightening the threadbare blanket around her legs.

'Oh, I don't know. My appetite isn't what it used to be, you know. I must have slept for quite some time,' she said, her voice groggy. 'How did work go today, Andrew?'

'Pretty good. They say the new desks and chairs will be in soon. That will make things more comfortable. Charles has left. Did I tell you? Heart attack. Too bad. I don't know how they are going to get on. They still owe a bundle on that old house. You'll have a little soup and I'll put you into your bed, okay?'

'Well, just a little, and no bread or crackers. How long have you been home, Andrew?'

'Just a while, June. Are you sure you won't have a slice of bread with me? It's from that French bakery? You love their rolls, don't you?'

'No, dear. The soup will be fine. How old is Charles?'

'Just sixty.'

'He used to come around, didn't he?'

'Not for years now.'

Then they were quiet. They were never much for long conversations. Stone added carrots to the steaming broth, put the heat on low and placed the lid on the pot. He took out two slices of brown bread for himself, spread some margarine on them and placed them on a chipped plate. A while later the soup was ready and he joined June in the sitting area and they ate in silence.

Andrew could see June was enjoying the soup and was happy for that. There were too few things that made her happy over the years. That was something he was going to change.

Andrew Stone felt that he was a failure in two ways. As a husband and as a provider. In the early years the couple had wanted children desperately and they eagerly awaited June getting pregnant. It didn't happen. Several years and doctors later, June had resigned herself to not having any babies. She even talked of adopting, but Andrew wouldn't hear of it. He refused to believe that he could not have any children and yet at the same time blamed himself for the barren marriage. After June developed polio, the idea of adoption died. They never discussed children again. But they both felt the deep sense of loss. Words just wouldn't have made things any better.

As a provider, Stone had always been faithful and steady. But to him, it was never enough. He dreamed of becoming an architect, creating things in his mind, on paper and in concrete. Andrew had dreamed also of the extra revenue and comfort such a career would earn them. June insisted he go to night school and she took the Woolworth's sales job to help pay for the courses. And she enjoyed the work.

He attended classes for several years, struggling with the workload, and balancing the factory and the classroom. A year after June's illness, after the wedding band had been pawned, he aborted the effort. The expense was too great and he couldn't leave June alone all those evenings. Again, they didn't talk much about it, but it was always there, something keeping both distant and close at the same time. With the passing of time, however, his reasoning became distorted and twisted until he believed he had actually quit out of laziness. This gave him another burden to carry. Andrew's job at the food plant paid for the rent, the prescriptions for June, the food and a new white shirt every six months, but little else. None of the comforts he desperately wanted to make June's lot an easier one. He was not happy with himself as a provider.

The couple bleakly finished their meal and then Andrew pushed June's chair to her bed and helped her into it. Next he brought a bowl, bar of soap, toothbrush, paste and towel and helped her wash up. He changed her into her pyjamas, helped with her bed pan, tucked her in and said goodnight.

The street was quiet on their corner where it met the system of back lanes he followed daily to work. Andrew Stone looked out the window for a moment and thought he felt older than he had ever felt before. He told himself that the quickening in his chest was connected to his anxiousness about getting the ring for June and he pushed away any suspicion he wouldn't have many more days to walk the alleyways of their town.

'I've got a few good years left in me yet,' he whispered.

Vigorously, he crossed the room to the cramped bathroom, washed himself, put out the lights and went to bed.

It was a sleepless night for Andrew Stone, but in the morning he was able to care for June, making her breakfast, setting her in her chair and covering her with the blanket before setting out to work. The volunteer nurse would bring her lunch and sit with her a while afterwards.

On his lunch break, Stone walked to the jewellery store to make the second last payment before picking up the ring. Once in the store he forgot how tired he was. Over in a corner, in a special velvet-lined box marked 'sold', sat the ring, an almost perfect replica of the original. Though he had seen it at least a dozen times now, the rich lustre and delicate handiwork still held Stone breathless. He thought of June slipping the ring joyfully on her finger. Stone could see her, green eyes sparkling, looking younger and more beautiful than ever. He fought off the temptation to grab it now, run home and give it to June today. But he would not take it out of the store until it was totally paid for. The jeweller, a timid man with spectacles, shook his head as Stone finally trudged slowly out of the door and back towards the plant for the afternoon shift, followed by the overtime cleaning job.

The jeweller checked his account book. Ten dollars more

and the old man would take the cheap ring home. One more day of gawking at it over his lunch time. One more day of handing over his wrinkled bills. He picked up the ring and fingered it gingerly in his expert hands. The cut of the engraving caught his eye. He had done a good job on that, he told himself. The letters were beautifully formed. The words, he thought, pathetically touching for an old man clearly on his last legs. Smiling, he read aloud.

'All my love.'

Funny, he didn't look like a poet. She probably wouldn't even be able to read it. The jeweller put down the ring, closed the case and went back to work, something of a sardonic smile on his face. It takes all kinds, he thought.

June Stone had few visitors to their room during the day other than the volunteer nurse. It had been years since anyone had come up to the dingy second floor. Years ago there was the old black woman with her Bible tracts. June remembered how the woman had made tea and toast for the two of them and had spoken about everything but the Bible. June had liked it that way. The big woman left hours later only just before Stone came home from work. June had been delighted with the way Andrew had asked questions later about the afternoon. It was as if they both had enjoyed the hours of chatting.

There were times also when Billy Bain from the plant would come and play gin with the Stones. That was during the evening and years ago now. Bain had since been let go because of his ill health and Andrew rarely saw him now. He used to make June laugh, though, as he made fun of the factory bosses while Andrew listened a little impatiently.

No one had been upstairs for years now. And for June Stone to receive two visitors in one day was in itself something very special.

At a little past two in the afternoon, she heard unfamiliar boots tramp up the stairs. She did not recognize Andrew's steps and was startled. The door was always open but she heard a knock and then the voice of O'Neil asking to be let in.

'I'm from the factory, ma'am. I have to speak to you about Andrew.'

That was the last word June heard – Andrew.

She was not listening as O'Neil looked at his feet as he quietly told her how Stone had collapsed at work. He spoke of how the plant nurse had desperately tried to revive him as he lay on the desk he had used for the past forty years. Stone was dead on arrival at the hospital, he told her.

June stared into space.

'There wasn't anything we could do, ma'am, just one of those things. We're all real upset about Andrew. Sorry for your loss, ma'am.'

He shifted his considerable weight from one foot to another as he spoke, and suddenly in mid-speech, took off the soiled hat he wore when on the plant floor, as if just then remembering the grim purpose of his visit.

'Of course, there is insurance provided by the company. You'll be alright for your medicines. I ... I'm sorry ma'am, there was nothing we could do. Stoney ... Andrew went real sudden, quick.'

Sunlight streamed into the drab room but June Stone could only barely make out the shape of O'Neil. He sensed this and wished he were somewhere else. Death is an awkward thing, he thought. He then placed Andrew's insurance policy and other papers on a table already stacked with newspapers. O'Neil stood waiting for a dismissal from a woman who hardly knew he was there.

Finally, he spoke again. 'It must have been the overtime. It's been four months now since the cleaner went away, problems over in Europe. Did he tell you about that? Well, of course he told you. I didn't want him to take that job. Too old. The young bucks should have taken it. They could have used the money to buy their girls something nice, flowers or chocolates. Or they could have fixed up their cars. But Stoney? What the hell did he want with the extra money? I don't know.'

He sensed himself talking more quickly now, as if releasing himself from any responsibility. He drew a deep breath and regained his composure.

'I'm sorry, ma'am,' he said, and walked out of the room, shutting the door behind him.

June Stone knew nothing of the overtime, the papers on the table, the ambulance, the plant nurse or the hospital. But she knew her Andrew was gone. She turned herself slightly in the chair, shifted her weight to the other side and stared once again out the window. It was raining and she could see the bulk of O'Neil heading down the familiar laneway, disappearing quickly in the mist.

Andrew had been a good man, she thought, one who tormented himself more than any God would dare. He had been a good provider, a good husband, a man who did his work soberly without complaining. She thought of the good times – of gently persuading him to take the architecture courses, listening as he dreamed aloud and talked of the pleasures that would come their way. And then she thought too of the difficult years when he would try to cheer them both up with his slow wit and dry encouragement.

'Well now, June, we'll get by, won't we?' he'd say in that sing-song way of his. 'We'll be alright, just you wait and see.'

Just you wait and see.

June Stone smiled to herself as tears sprinkled on to her lap.

It seemed darker as June let her head drop for sleep, putting off how she would get on in the future. The care home would be ready for her, she knew, though she worried how she would pay. She would need plenty of energy facing her days now without Andrew. She would definitely have to move, but she would not think about that just yet. Now she just wanted to close her eyes and dream of her Andrew, her husband who never let her down, who always made her happy.

But sleep wouldn't come. Something was bothering her. Do you suppose, she wondered, that Andrew knew she was happy all these years? She became panicky with this new thought. Had he killed himself trying to get more for her when she was already happy enough with what she had? Did she tell him this?

This time June's tears were bitter and stung her eyes. The tears were for Andrew and they came faster and lasted a long time.

The second visitor climbed the stairs quietly and June barely heard the knock on her door. She turned to see him walk through the door.

'Are you Mrs Andrew Stone?' he asked stiffly.

She nodded. More bad news? Surely not.

'I have something for you.'

He handed her the package and was about to turn and leave when he saw the distress in the old woman's eyes. Then the jeweller began to speak, though he hardly knew what he was saying.

'He was a very special man, your husband, Mrs Stone. I bet you didn't even know what he was planning. And this ring, or giving it to you, at least, must have meant an awful lot to him. He came by the store often, you know. Paid promptly too, every week. He could have had it from the beginning, you know. I trusted him. But no, he wanted it paid for one hundred percent. That's the way he said it. Of course, there's one week's payment owing, but I won't worry about that. Not now . . .'

Then he was quiet and watched her smile and he noticed the green of her eyes. They were lovely and he thought for a moment he was looking at a young woman in full bloom. He found himself blushing and suddenly began to make his exit.

'I'm sorry about Mr Stone. He was a good man.'

Then he disappeared out the door.

After a long moment, June Stone clumsily opened her wrapped parcel and gently pulled apart the velvet box, dropping the tiny ring into her palm. She closed her fist and held it close to her.

'Thank you,' she said aloud. 'Thank you for everything.'

She placed the ring on her finger and it fit snugly just as before. Then she was young again. Her eyes were filled with tears and their green sparkled.

Mad Summer

It was the most sweltering of a string of sticky July days when Uncle Harry suddenly packed his few personal belongings into a grey tote bag and walked out of the Tranquillity Nursing Residence that had been his address for the past decade.

He left on his own; didn't call a cab; didn't say anything to his son, the downtown corporate lawyer; and even managed to avoid informing his daughter, the busy housewife who visited him every three days like clockwork.

Uncle Harry, who was at that time just one month shy of his eightieth birthday, did, however, make one phone call before leaving Tranquillity.

Just after breakfast, Uncle Harry cradled the blue touch tone in his lap and began staring at it fearfully. On the table in front of him was a small piece of paper with seven digits on it. He knew the numbers by heart but feared that he would misdial when the moment came.

When his lunch tray arrived, he waved the server away. He couldn't eat. The knots in his stomach were so tight it felt like he had somehow grown a new appendix sixty years after the useless piece of tissue had been wrenched from his guts during surgery.

Uncle Harry's eyes were running like a leaky toilet and he kept dabbing them with a tissue that was more than a little worse for wear. And the stringy old goat, who had seen so many summers like this one that his friends and relatives wondered just how many more he would see, felt for all the world like he was just fourteen years old – all that nervous, sweaty anxiety that both scared the devil out of him and reminded him that there truly was a God. And there wasn't much he could do about this feeling either – other than maybe put down the phone. But he wasn't about to do that – not this time.

At 3:30 p.m., Uncle Harry finally cast out his demons and picked up the telephone. He shook his grey-bearded face to and fro a moment, whispered a near silent prayer ('God, I hope you, at least, know what you're doing.') and dialled the number.

When he hung up a few minutes later, Uncle Harry left the neat, clean predictability of Tranquillity.

Those who saw him that evening as climbed the Ham Hill noted there was something of a spring in his step. They wondered if they could hear him singing under his breath, something nasally, maybe Country and Western. But they were appalled at the sight of his face. His eyes were moist, his mouth rigid in determination and his brow furrowed like a farmer's field.

*

Uncle Harry never had wanted to move out of the house. It was the downtown lawyer and the overly attentive housewife who convinced him he couldn't handle it any more. He figured they were tired of his calls, asking them to pick up groceries or hardware so he could continue tinkering with old motors in his garage. He couldn't drive since the accident that killed his wife Joan just before his sixty-fifth birthday.

But Uncle Harry had gone along with the move. Tranquillity sounded enticing somehow and the corporate lawyer and the busy housewife promised him he would meet people his own age.

Imagine their shock, then, when one week after Uncle Harry moved back into the old place on the Ham Hill, Beth, beautiful and barely 30, walked up the front steps, shook the dust off her shoes, brushed her hair back with painted fingers, went in and closed the door behind her.

*

The first one to visit Uncle Harry and his 'young friend', as the gossiping chorus referred to the tiny vivacious Beth, was Pastor Hurley, the chaplain from Tranquillity. It was hot as hell and Hurley was wearing his clerical collar. Little pools of sweat gathered on his neck, but he wouldn't take off the stiff collar.

'Look, Harry, sure she's young, she's beautiful, she's passionate, she's sexy, she's in love with you and, if I do say so myself, she has a depth of spiritual longing that exceeds anything I have found in the church, but . . .'

'Jesus, Hurley, this is how you try and convince me to give her up? And they say I'm the mad one!'

He fixed Hurley with the kind of glare that made the little chaplain think he could see into his very soul. Hurley was unnerved.

Truth was that Hurley was in love with Beth himself, not that he was able to say it straight up. Uncle Harry, who knew the comings and goings at Tranquillity as well as anyone, was well aware of this and waited for Hurley to declare it. But that didn't happen.

*

Beth began working at Tranquillity as a sixteen-year-old volunteer when she was still in high school. She would bring around magazines, do some light cleaning and look after the small comforts of the residents like Uncle Harry, who were pretty independent but sometimes needed a little extra tender loving care. Beth had one of those honest to goodness smiles that was so infectious it got everyone around her feeling better. She was a real joy to have around Tranquillity. And Beth just loved being part of the place – connecting to all those folks who felt abandoned, and listening to their stories while she dusted, cleaned the bathrooms and posted cards to family members.

Uncle Harry loved to tell stories. He had been a magazine

writer back when he was in his twenties and thirties, churning out travel pieces for all the good magazines that have given way to those purveyors of puff, the kind where you can't tell the difference between the perfume and booze ads and the feature articles.

With his white eyebrows arching towards the sky, Uncle Harry would transform the stock and trade travel tales of cruising the Caribbean, mountain climbing in the Alps and caboose riding through the Rocky Mountains with his witty anecdotes and self-deprecating one liners (mostly about getting lost), and the grisly old fart would punctuate those tales with fibs about editors who were so drunk they couldn't see straight and fellow writers who couldn't spell worth a damn.

Even before she returned to Tranquillity as a nurse, the slim, brown-haired Beth had a way of listening to Uncle Harry's stories that kept her from being a supplicant transfixed at the feet of a master. She was nobody's fool. She listened to the story but also to the inflections in his dramatic voice, while watching the wrinkling of his forehead, the body language. All the while, Beth would keep a keen eye on whether Uncle Harry was comfortable in his little corner of Tranquillity. It came natural for her. She did it for all the residents, but she gradually spent more and more time with the storied old gentleman.

*

The next visitor to the little house on the Ham Hill was the chair of the board of the Presbyterian Church of Ham Hill, where Uncle Harry and Aunt Joan had been charter members. Mrs Irwin Perkins was short, stout and full of righteous anger. Ham Hill Presbyterian was known as the most liberal of the area's Presbyterian churches but not when it came to matters of the flesh. There, they were as conservative as the best Baptists.

Mrs Perkins arrived at the beginning of August with a neatly typed memo in hand. She had written it herself and then had taken it to the special meeting of the board for consideration after a service that had attracted just a handful of ageing worshippers. Within minutes of the end of the service, the board had accepted the contents of the memo. She volunteered to deliver it to Uncle Harry in person.

She started curtly.

'We the board of the Presbyterian Church of Ham Hill do on this third day of August 1985 call on Harold Johnson charter member of this congregation to resign from this congregation until such time as he is able to renounce his sinful relationship which has not been blessed by either church or state.'

Mrs Perkins looked up from her memo, feeling very satisfied with her efforts. Then she handed it to Uncle Harry.

After perusing it himself, Uncle Harry broke into one of his trademark grins, 'God, you sure could use an editor on that board. Your grammar and punctuation are pathetic,' he laughed.

Beth, sitting beside Uncle Harry on the settee, picked up her book of short stories and began reading again.

There was nothing more to say. Mrs Perkins left. Uncle Harry picked up his tea with one hand and reached over and rubbed Beth's stiff shoulder with the other.

'That feels good,' she said, turning her neck to watch his pockmarked hand rub her young shoulder. 'You don't know how good that feels.'

'I have a suspicion,' he responded.

*

Even when she was studying nursing, Beth found time to put in a few hours a month volunteering at Tranquillity. She was bright and her studies went well, and Beth had a special gift that let her patients feel better about their predicament.

'She has healing ways,' her teachers would say.

Beth fell madly in love with an architect from the city before she graduated from nursing college. She finished her courses but never sought out a job in any of the local hospitals so she could marry Matt and look after his home in the city. It turned out Matt wanted a maid, a mother for his two children and a caterer for his regular business dinners, which he threw to keep his contacts well fed and lubricated. Matt was married to his business and took to the drink in a serious way.

Beth was nobody's fool, but when it came to matters of the heart, she had a certain naiveté. However, within a year she realized she had made a terrible mistake. She fled the big city, the marriage and all the domestic responsibilities, a wounded but stronger woman. She took some time off then fought herself back into shape. She was ready to nurse again.

Tranquillity was looking for a nurse just as Beth returned to town. Beth was hired immediately. Staff and residents were ecstatic.

*

Doctor Willis then came to visit Uncle Harry and Beth at the Ham Hill house. Uncle Harry's son and daughter had paid him a call at his office in the new strip mall on the east end of town.

'This just doesn't make sense,' the daughter cried, waving her hands in frustration. 'I'm sure he has completely lost his mind.'

'What exactly are you worried about?' the ancient family doctor asked. 'Do you think he will hurt himself? Do you think she will abscond with the family fortune? Come on, it's just a fling.'

Doctor Willis didn't pay much attention to the arm waving or the extravagant language but heard the concern of the two offspring and promised to pay a call.

Doctor Willis was no pushover. He had a slow, quiet way about him that had fooled more than one young member of the local academy of medicine over the years when they had attempted to challenge him on hospital privileges.

Uncle Harry was alone the day Doctor Willis arrived on his doorstep. It was coffee time and Doctor Willis joined Uncle Harry for a cup, although Uncle Harry made it too strong for his taste.

Doctor Willis and Uncle Harry weren't close but they went back a long way and had an easy way of relating.

'So, the kids tell me you've been home about a month now. How's it been going?'

'You're the doctor, Doc, how do you think I look?'

'Truth is, you don't look all that bad for a man your age.'

They both laughed at that.

'I guess the kids think I've gone mad and taken up with some kind of gold-digging nymphomaniac?'

'Something like that. How do you see it?'

Uncle Harry was uncharacteristically quiet.

After a long pause, he spoke. Doctor Willis silently sipped the bitter black coffee.

'I have not lost my mind. I know precisely what I am doing. After a lifetime of looking after my family, I made a decision that would make almost no one happy, except for me and Beth. Do you know how hard that was for someone with my neurotic character flaws?'

Doctor Willis laughed. 'Okay,' he said.

'The thing that's crazy is that it has taken me until I was almost eighty years of age to fall in love – I mean really head over heels in love. You know I loved Joan all those years, but it was a low boil. I'm not complaining, but this with Beth, well, it's like out of this world. I want to be with her morning, noon and night. She always looks beautiful to me. We read together, we walk all over Ham Hill, we discuss everything and, hell, we have a better sex life than I ever imagined possible – ever.'

Uncle Harry fixed his eyes on Doctor Willis.

'And that's what's pissing them off – the kids, Hurley, Perkins, the whole tight-assed congregation and probably some of my neighbours here, who I notice have stopped coming out on their porches when Beth and I are out here.'

'Yeah, there is a difference in our ages, although I couldn't tell you the exact number of years. But bloody hell, Doc, we have more love and affection between us than most married couples born within a month of each other.'

Uncle Harry was by now a little agitated and the sweat began to pour off his patchy brow. He went into the old house to mop up and get himself some more of his special brew of coffee.

Doctor Willis just sat in silence, a slight grin on his face.

By the time Uncle Harry came back out to the porch several minutes later, Doctor Willis was in his car, waving goodbye out the window.

'See you later, Harry, I've got sick people to visit.'

When Beth arrived home from the afternoon shift at Tranquillity, she carried a legal envelope and wore an ominous expression.

'It seems,' she started gingerly, 'Tranquillity has this policy in its personnel fine print that says that staff members shouldn't become "overly involved in the lives of their patients" and that overly involved is determined by the "family of the patients or the administrator", so I no longer have a job there as a registered nurse.'

'Sounds like my darlings have been talking to administration.'

'More than just talking,' Beth responded.

Uncle Harry and Beth moved silently together for a long, tearful embrace. Finally, his lips found hers and they kissed fiercely for a full minute. They moved into the bedroom and spent the next two hours alternately holding each other, stroking each other and resting.

The next morning Beth went out to buy a newspaper to study the classifieds while Uncle Harry puttered in the garage. He was stiff and sore from the night before, but invigorated.

At noon, the corporate lawyer and the busy housewife arrived. Uncle Harry sat in his favourite old living room chair, ready to listen, but resolved not to budge.

'Dad,' his daughter began, 'we just think you are making the worst mistake of your life, moving out of Tranquillity and living with ... Beth. She's too young. Dad, you're too old. It's just not ... seemly.'

She waited for him to respond but he didn't.

Uncle Harry's son took up the cause. 'Do you know enough about her background? Has she ever done this before? Does she have money of her own? I mean, my concern here is—'

Uncle Harry finally interrupted.

'She *did* have a well-paying job – up until yesterday when Tranquillity found some bullshit *legal* reason to push her out the door.'

He stared at his son.

'Dad,' the now-flushed son continued, 'we're concerned you may not be ... uh ... able to draw on all your mental faculties, worried that you are not fully ...'

'What did Doctor Willis tell you?' Harry wanted to know.

'Dad, we've started legal proceedings and will be dealing with a new doctor.'

'Fuck. Why can't you leave me alone? Have you ever actually considered my happiness in all this? All you've done is get out your bloody slide rulers and figured in your logical way that Dad is too old, that Beth is too young. Have you ever thought that I might just have all my marbles and be topsy-turvy in love? Sure, she's young and I'm old, but at this moment I swear we have more in common than you two do with me. Have you forgotten what it is to fall in love?'

Uncle Harry was aware of the state of the love lives of both his offspring and felt a twinge of guilt over that comment. 'I really need a rest and would like the two of you the hell out of here now.'

With that, he left the room to go lie down in the bedroom. The corporate lawyer and the busy housewife left the house in silence.

Beth returned a few hours later, her red-circled newspaper under her arm. She found two blue leather suitcases sitting on the porch. Uncle Harry was in the bathroom gathering up some of his toiletries. A two-tone taxi arrived but Beth gave the confused driver a couple of dollars and asked him to disappear.

When Uncle Harry emerged red-eyed from the bathroom, Beth sat him down at the kitchen table, stared directly at his shaggy grey face.

'What's this all about?'

Before Uncle Harry could answer, she continued. It was her turn to talk.

'I know you love me. I feel it in my shoulders when you massage them. I hear it in your heartbeat when you hold me. I sense it in your eyes when you look at me. There are no other hard realities, just complications we can overcome. And you know I love you. This love we have is unlike anything I have ever experienced in my long life.' She laughed. 'And I'm not going to let any doctors, lawyers or anxious kids spoil it. If you want to show how mad you are, walk out that door. Otherwise, I'm going to bed.'

She concluded with a smile that was dead serious and a kiss that didn't exactly hit its target.

Uncle Harry sat a long while, tears welling up in his eyes. He had never in his life felt more loved, more alive.

He went into the bedroom and closed the door.

It was a night like no other. No noise, no talk, no lovemaking, at least not in the traditional sense. Uncle Harry and Beth just held each other, so tightly they became one. It was a fusion no church or state could fashion, but it was real and life-giving.

For Uncle Harry, it was the best way possible to spend his last few hours on the earth. He died in his early-morning sleep and Beth felt it in the midst of hers. She woke quietly and covered her beloved man.

Pastor Hurley did a fine funeral for Uncle Harry. Most of the mobile folks from Tranquillity were there and so were a number from the Presbyterian Church of Ham Hill, including Mrs Perkins and some of the board.

*

My father was too sick to travel to the funeral of his dear brother and asked me to attend on his behalf.

Afterwards, I looked for Beth but didn't see her in the church. With all the smut I had heard in the past month or so, my curiosity got the better of me and I walked the few blocks from the church to my Uncle Harry's little house on the Ham Hill.

Beth invited me in immediately. I was expecting to see a young woman, if not distraught, at least in mourning. She was anything but, and, as if reading my mind, pointed to the giant painted flower on her T-shirt.

'Your Uncle Harry loved flowers and he warned me not to wear black on the day of his funeral,' she said, her eyes bright as sunshine.

'How come you didn't go?' I asked her.

'I had nothing to mourn. We knew we wouldn't last forever. Believe it or not, I wasn't so sure that Harry would die first. He was so vigorous.'

A beatific smile crossed her face.

'Didn't you feel cheated by him dying so suddenly?'

'The timing of Harry's death didn't cheat me. I still feel his arms around me. I'll never forget the way he looked at me and talked to me, the care he gave to me in words and other ways. I didn't ask him for a time line, just a love line. And I got it.'

I sat for a while in admiration of this tiny woman; and of my Uncle Harry, a man I clearly should have got to know better; and of the possibility that love of this kind could survive the plots against it.

I got up to leave and was halfway down the porch steps when I decided to ask one more question.

'They say he was mad, you know, out of his mind. What do you think, Beth?'

She broke into a broad smile. 'Are you kidding? Hell, he was as mad as a hatter.'

She laughed loudly as she shut the door.

'Then the whole world needs a little more madness,' I whispered under my breath. 'The whole world ought to go mad for a summer.'

The Geneva Convention

I didn't sleep with her.

I know, you've heard this before. I have a reputation: richly deserved, too many dark nights when I was so lonesome that I embraced any comfort I could find. Too many broken promises, arriving home to the pure white sheets of my marriage with the faint scent of bodily secretions mixed with perfume about me, hoping my gracefully sleeping wife, her back a kind of Berlin wall down the middle of the bed, would not notice. Hoping against hope for another chance. That this was not the fatal fling, the unforgivable mortal sin. And then too many times when I left your bed to try one more time to fix another broken love with the fury of desperate, sweaty mating, this time arriving home to your piercing glances over the top of those half-moon glasses that remained fixed on Dickens, Eliot or the latest pale attempt of your students to emulate. But it's true. I really didn't sleep with her. She was a friend. My very good friend, the kind of friend that happens by accident at first but gets nourished with steaming hot tea and biscuits, glasses of white wine, misty late-night walks through ancient narrow streets, music and the trading of books, good books; and with being clear.

'I am not looking for a husband or lover.'

I can still see her saying that now, raising that wild Irish eyebrow, ever the serious diplomat, woman of substance, while responding to my question.

'Are you sure?'

Then came her response, characteristically succinct. 'Absolutely.' The extra lilt of her accent serving as the exclamation point at the end of her declaration. Her piercing eyes looking into my soul, as if to beg her own question. 'But are *you* sure?'

Then, picking up the dark-framed reading glasses she wore around her neck, she'd continue to peruse the bilingual menu in one of the many dimly lit cafes we frequented within walking distance of her tiny one-bedroom flat in downtown Geneva.

I am not really sure I can speak to her state of mind the night (early morning, actually) that we met. I suspect she was letting off a little steam after another gruelling week of high-level meetings at the World Health Organization, some going well past midnight with early-morning starts the next day. It is the life of the Geneva diplomatic, workaholic corps. She was with her colleague Connie (her real name was Condoleezza but she never admitted to that), a brash African-American whose voice and southern accent were like sweet syrup to the ear.

'I may be Baptist, honey, but I ain't Southern Baptist. Let's not take a good thing too far,' she would drawl.

I had been wandering from bar to bar, looking for God knows what or God knows who, knowing enough in my head to stay away from the demon booze that took my father to his early grave but enjoying the newly found freedom of not having to worry about driving a car under the influence since I was car-less in Geneva. I had been by the Leopard Room, which is located in the swanky Hotel Angleterre in downtown Geneva overlooking Lake Geneva (or as the locals call it, Lac Lemain), a few times and thought it looked like a cosy little hideaway, similar to ones I had frequented in Toronto, like the old piano bar, the Silver Rail, or in my adopted hometown Kitchener, the Library Lounge. It was a hideaway, but for who? Was it for slick men with secret stashes of ill-gotten gain? Or women avoiding a love gone wrong? I wondered as I gingerly grabbed the handrail taking me down the stairs to the Leopard Room, leopard patterns on every wall, wild animal ashtrays, and plush couches with patterned cushions. And a beautiful black man at the piano, his voice pure ivory, crooning like Sinatra.

I ordered a Heineken, maybe another. The music stopped and Connie, two stools over at the bar, hauled me over to discuss the beautiful singer, and before I knew it, I was guessing whose accent came from where and discussing the state of American and world politics; another lousy American election was in the offing and it looked like the forces of evil would win yet again. It seemed like a bit of a dream, that time at the Leopard Room. Perhaps there was another Heineken. And soon the lovely Irish diplomat, Sheila, in the beautifully cut suit that snugly fit her compact body quietly handed me her card, as if to say, 'This is real' and jolt me out of my alcoholic haze. Then we were off to another bar and another, wandering the streets at three in the morning, dodging hookers and johns and shielding our eyes from the garish storefront lights that proclaimed SEX. 'Subtle,' I thought. Connie and Sheila were wearing flashing red devil's horns in honour of Halloween and giggling like schoolgirls looking for candy. I was hungry.

'I want fries,' my thick tongue managed and soon enough we were sitting on Sheila's couch munching on fries she had retrieved from the freezer while I perused her bookshelves, muttering (I thought to myself). 'Iris Murdoch, Noam Chomsky, oh my God, you really read.'

And Connie kept proclaiming, 'Yeah, you guys would be great together, both great readers.'

And I couldn't look at anyone and wondered if I had said something about what I had been reading, hoped to hell I hadn't drunkenly claimed to be a writer and that I wouldn't have to now explain how I hadn't written a word, other than internal memos to my boss at the Red Cross Museum, for years.

Oh God.

I hated those Sunday afternoons in Geneva. They only brought darkness, gloom, the guilt of having drunk too much or said too much or fallen asleep on someone's couch or in a stairwell the night before; and dread over the week to come. This Sunday afternoon I fought all that off and tried to retrace the steps of the night before. I couldn't find where Sheila lived. I couldn't find the second or third bars of the night before, I couldn't even find the SEX shops. I did find the Leopard Room. I peered in the locked door. The piano was silent, the ashtrays clean. No drinks were being spilled. Not a soul was in sight. What in God's name was I looking for, anyway? I'm not really sure, even today, but I think I wanted another chance to talk to this nurse turned diplomat with the wide Irish smile. I wanted to see whether she really did have that gift of conversation, true engagement, whether words fell from her lips like spring water in a tumbling brook; whether she really looked you in the eye when you were talking and heard you. Or I wanted to find out it was just the beer, go home and forget about her. I stuck my hand in my worn leather jacket and pulled out Sheila's business card, grabbed my mobile and called. No one was there to put me through to her voice mail.

I went home and tested the old hair-of-the-dog theory.

The next day dawned with me nursing a nervous gut and my hands cold and clammy, but I knew I had to send her a message.

Dear Sheila: It was great to run into you at the Leopard Room Saturday night and then to enjoy the hospitality of tea and chips and books at your flat. While it is true that I have a relationship back in Canada, I was wondering if we could meet again sometime as friends to talk, sip a cup of tea or better, walk, go the movies, a concert. If I don't hear from you, I will understand that you are saying no thanks. Cheers, Marcus.

I went to the office toilet, threw up, came back to my desk and hit send on my computer.

Hours later I received Sheila's reply.

Dear Marcus: It was good to meet you too. You need to know that while I had a good time Saturday night, this is not my normal weekend protocol. I appreciate your offer and I am delighted to answer in the affirmative. Get in touch and make a suggestion. Sheila Connor.

And so, just days later in the smoky Leopard Room, the same lovely singer continued his world tour, to Jamaica where the nights are gay.

And we picked up our conversation from the other night.

'Why did you agree to this?'

Sheila, the diplomat, wearing a blue pinstripe suit over a ruffled silk blouse, her reddish brown hair closely cropped, looked somehow smaller but more athletic than I remembered.

'I just figured anyone who made such a fuss over my books might be interesting enough to meet again.'

And so it started, the talk, the laughter, the agreement to meet again soon, the clumsy first Swiss kiss, touching cheeks three times.

She was married very young. Still in nursing school, she did the inevitable, fell for a handsome doctor, and they were married three months later, happy ostensibly for twenty years, until he announced one day that he had fallen in love with the receptionist Sheila knew only as Yvonne, the blonde who was constantly filing her shapely nails whenever she visited the office. He was gone in an hour, leaving few traces in their comfortable London home other than the two young boys now clinging to their mother's tear-stained skirt. Sheila was devastated but only a few very close friends knew it. She poured herself into more studies, getting her Masters in international studies and diplomacy, a move that bought her a ticket out of town. There were a couple of relationships over the years, at least a couple that she told me about. One was actually a racing-car driver with a garage full of fancy cars. The only thing good about that relationship was the sex. She told this me one humid evening on the patio of one of our favourite Italian spots in the old town.

'I have no regrets, eighteen months of great sex and feeling like an attractive woman.'

Another time she told me there had been a very brief relationship in Geneva with a colleague. She could see my eyes squint as I went through a mental list of the men I knew who worked with her and she smiled.

'Forget it, you don't know him. Anyway, he lives in India now.'

Was that a touch of regret I heard in her voice? It didn't matter now. The white wine was good that night. Later the Irish pub was smoky and crowded, and we laughed about almost everything – her kids, mine, and some of the week's work blunders.

It's not as if I was never tempted. So many times walking the downtown streets of Geneva, looking for the best Thai or Arabic restaurant, I started to reach out to put my arm around her and stopped. Many days I almost grabbed her hand as you do instinctively with a long-time partner as we walked briskly around the lake. (Nurses always walk quickly, she told me. 'That's part of the training.') I remember once riding the tram to the local Latin American film festival when she stumbled towards me and her forehead touched my chin. I started to move my lips towards hers, like you move to scratch an itch, but stopped. She smiled. We went to Paris one weekend and stayed at a friend's apartment. We stayed up late drinking French wine and discussing the latest Geneva-set Paulo Coelho novel and I found myself thinking of her in my arms, in my bed, removing my clothes. But it was just a flash, a little too much wine. We didn't want it that way. I was flying back and forth to you at Christmas and in the summer. She was convinced the single life was for her. She had a great circle of friends, men and women. She never lacked for a companion to go with her to a concert or the movies or supper. If she ever pined for a lover or husband or even a fling, she didn't tell me. She was happy with being single.

One cold January afternoon I received an email message from Sheila at my desk at the museum.

> *Marcus: I am being transferred to London immediately. I will be back in Geneva in a month for a farewell and to clean out my flat. Sorry, no time for even a drink before I leave. I'll explain in another note. All the best, Sheila.*

The WHO held a farewell in a quiet green solarium off the Leopard Room. Most of the folks attending were from the diplomatic corps. There were a few of us who were friends Sheila had met along the way. I wondered how she met them. Could the circumstances be as bizarre as our meeting? Her boss at the WHO, a beautiful blonde doctor from Russia with sad eyes and the most fabulous array of fur coats, gave a nice speech about loyalty and dedication. One of her colleagues handed her a dozen roses but was too teary to say much, other than how much she would miss the early-morning walks, skiing in the Alps and tea at Sheila's flat during a particularly difficult time in her marriage.

My speech went something like this:

'Sheila is my very dear friend. One of the very few women I have been fortunate to get close to and not marry or move in with. She is the kind of friend who insists your worst stories are not boring, tells you you're are a good listener, shows up when you have the worst cold with a whiskey recipe that nearly kills you. She is the kind of friend who comes when you tell her a dear colleague has died suddenly and you need some quiet company. She is the kind of friend who shows up with a first aid kit and patches up your face and bends your glasses back in shape when you've had a fall and doesn't ask whether you had been drinking. She is also the kind of friend who knows just when to ask: "But did you learn anything from it" when you know you have screwed up badly. She is the kind of friend you miss.'

It was a great speech, really, but I didn't actually get to deliver it. There was supposed to be an open-mike time when folks could wander up and talk about Sheila, but after an awkward few moments where I couldn't find the strength or breath to get on my feet, someone turned the music up loud and the party started anew.

There were a few connections and missed opportunities to meet over the years. I was back in Canada, back in your bed with all its blissful scents and opportunities. She was in London. I got an email out of the blue one Friday when I was leaving the university where I worked as an assistant researcher. She would be in Ottawa on the weekend. Here is the address and phone number. Call me, visit, whatever you can, she said. You were grading papers so off I went. But it was January and I got stuck in a snowstorm near Peterborough and had to pull off the road and into a motel. I called the number she gave but no one answered.

Another time I was in London doing some research at the Museum of History when I was able to reach Sheila at her new office in the Department of Health where she served as a deputy minister and she invited me to her birthday party at a local pub near her workplace that very night. I arrived just as a clutch of well-dressed colleagues were singing a little drunkenly, 'Happy Birthday to you . . .' A few moments later as I was at the bar getting myself a pint of Kilkenny, she came up beside me and gave me the familiar Swiss kiss. We laughed about our last attempt to get together in Ottawa, got caught up on our children's exploits and toasted future meetings. Then a red-haired colleague named Alice, who had been drinking heavily and was slurring her words, pulled the birthday girl away so she could meet her new love interest, an Aussie with the widest grin and a totally shaved head. I tried to connect with her a few more times that night as the birthday revellers began to mix with the general Friday-night pub crowd in a delicious dance that reminded me of a dog park in a wealthy neighbourhood, where fancy puppies would sniff a well-coiffed poodle or terrier and then move on to friendlier territory. But she remained occupied by a coterie of colleagues in well-cut suits, and frankly she was having a grand time and I loved watching her in that light. At midnight I left the pub, only to catch a glimpse of Sheila stepping into a cab with a very tall dark-haired man, carrying an umbrella and a fat briefcase.

There were a few emails over the next few years but they were brief. She was moving back to Ireland. She was a grandmother again. She had a health scare but all was well. I told her you had retired, that I was between contracts. We promised to have a telephone conversation around Christmas but it just didn't happen. I was going crazy finishing a project and I presumed she was enjoying the good life of a retiree and grandmother.

In January I got a telephone call from her son Patrick, just as I was stepping out of the shower to face the day.

She was gone. Cancer. The uterus.

'Fuck,' I said as I slammed the receiver down.

The flight to Dublin was uneventful. I bent over the little food tray and scribbled furiously on Air Canada napkins. The funeral was in an old church near the botanical gardens. It was bursting at the seams with well-dressed mourners in blacks and greys. There was the sweet scent of flowers and perfume. The priest, a family friend, spoke with the ease and grace of a poet about 'our lovely Sheila.' One of her sons, Matthew, read a letter that Sheila had written to the family. Her former husband sat not far from me in the back row of the dark old church, his head bowed.

Again there was an open mike.

I didn't want to miss this opportunity again, so I was at the microphone before anyone else. My Air Canada napkins stayed in the pew.

'My name is Marcus Best. I am a friend of Sheila's from Canada. We got to be good friends when we were both posted to Geneva years ago.'

The priest shuffled his feet behind me and I turned to make sure he wasn't coming to whisk me away. He smiled benignly. Someone coughed nervously.

'But we did develop a kind of closeness that I wanted to talk about for a few moments here this morning.'

Someone tittered.

I carried on.

'If you asked Sheila Connor about herself, she would be quick to tell you about all her limitations. She was too short. She couldn't cook. Her French was terrible. But if you ask her friends to describe her, they will use words like loyal, dedicated, optimistic or honest. I just want to add this: She was my friend. She took me the way I was, not when it suited her but always; she never judged me even though I messed up many times over the years we knew each other.'

They were looking at me now, dew-eyed.

I continued.

'She taught me that men and women could be friends without being lovers.'

I paused. A man in the front row cleared his throat. And the good Father stood up and put his arm around me.

'We thank our Canadian friend for his kind words about our Sheila.'

And this time I was whisked away.

Putting on my overcoat at the back of the church, I felt a tap on my shoulder. It was Patrick, his youngest, Patricia, wrapped around his shoulders, burying her grief in her father's warm shoulder. He took my hand and his dark eyes fixed mine for a solid minute before he spoke.

'Mom said you were her true friend.'

And he was gone.

On the flight back to Toronto I closed my eyes, pretending to be asleep so that I wouldn't be disturbed with bad airline food or worse movies. Every now and then I dabbed my eyes with my Air Canada napkin.

Tea for Three

The boyish doctor at my local surgery delivered the news in his usual straightforward manner on a wet Friday afternoon. Peering over his half-glasses while I sat in silent disbelief in his cramped office, he spoke without emotion.

'Your heart is failing rather rapidly, Jackson. I'm afraid the best-case scenario is . . .'

That's all I heard.

I went home to my tidy flat above the Mexican restaurant off the high street, shut the door behind me, drew the curtains and stared at the telephone for the entire weekend.

On Monday I emerged again, only slightly encouraged by the way the sun hit the church steeple out on the heath. I did some shopping for groceries at Costcutters, knowing Alice would be shaking her head in dismay at my choice of shops if she were still alive.

Then I saw the posters while rummaging through the dusty bookstore near the heath:

'Sisters – like branches on a tree, we grow differently; remain rooted in shared history.'

The words were printed in simple black script on a matted rust background next to a photograph of two Native American women sitting side-by-side at a glass lake. I bought the pair of them and struggled home with the posters and my bag of bread, milk and currant buns.

At home, I printed two little cards on my clunking printer. One said: 'From Angela'; the other read: 'From Barb.' Then I sent the posters to my two sisters, who live at opposite ends of London, and went to the pub, where I can look across the heath and see the winking Canary Wharf from my favourite window seat, and ordered an Old Speckled Hen. My sisters would soon have their gifts from each other. I drank that thought in with a long draught of cold beer.

My sisters haven't spoken to one another for forty years.

Angela

I am returning the ridiculous thing you sent. What possessed you to make an assumption of closeness after all this time?

Barb

We grew up in Canada, each of us journeying to London over the intervening years. I met my wife Alice on the Toronto Island ferry. I was dead drunk from a night of partying after the Mariposa Folk Festival. Rambling Jack Elliott had been howling out Woody Guthrie songs and bragging how he had taught Bob Dylan to sing. Alice took me in, and a few months later we moved to London, her hometown. My sisters followed years later for their own reasons.

When Angela was sixteen she decided she was going to be a nun. It was 1966 and Toronto the Good was prim and proper. We have always called her Angel. One of our lovely aunts sent her a birthday card with a pop-out pink birthday cake and inadvertently dropped the final 'a' and it stuck. Angel. She had shock-red hair and a mischievous left eye that twitched. She was always with lads down at the beach, hiking in the woods, running away from home with her rabbit's foot and sweat socks tucked into Father's duffle bag, coaxing me and Barb into all manner of mischief. She got us to take a 'holiday' from delivering the afternoon *Star* up the steep inclines of our neighbourhood because it was 'a great day for a picnic' by the lifeguard station at the beach. It was, in fact, a freezing cold and windy March afternoon and we shivered against one another, sipping Orange Crush from paper straws and eating salty crisps. Father was furious, cursing as he drove us around the paper route at the end of his long day patching the city's roads, while his supper simmered at home.

'Woe betide you when I get you home,' he roared when we were finally crammed into the old Chev. Usually, Mother would be able to calm him when we got home.

Barb

Is this some kind of sick joke after all these years? I am sending the damned poster back. We were never that close; pretending at this late stage is pathetic.

Angela

Barb actually looked the angel part; pretty and blonde with peachy cheeks, she was blessed with a sweet smile. They didn't allow altar girls so she joined the church choir and the Girl Guides. Barb was too straight-laced to get up to much trouble. When she did, Mother and Father knew she had been coerced by Angel. Barb grew up quickly; she was the first with breasts swelling under her colourful jumpers; she wore makeup when it was still a sin; there were rumours that a boy had touched her while walking home from a church dance. But there was only ever speculation about sex. I sure as hell was in the dark about it back then.

Angela

What is going on? I just mailed the poster to you and got it back. Stop this nonsense. It's too late.

Barb

Barb fell in love with Father Anthony at our church across from the racetrack. Father Anthony was as tall as God, with big bushy eyebrows and a beatific smile. Barb would sit and watch him on the church tennis courts, anticipating every lunge for the ball that exposed those long brown legs against his crisp white shorts. She would linger after games but could barely utter a word. Father Anthony would just stroll by her on his way to the rectory like Jimmy Connors, mopping his forehead with his white towel.

'Hello there, Barb. How's that backswing of yours? Keep working on it.'

'Yes, Father Anthony. I'm working on it. Bye, Father Anthony,' she mumbled to her white tennis shoes.

Barb

You're right. Stop sending the poster.

Angela

Angel's desire to be a nun caused a seismic quake in the household. Mother and Father were on different sides of the fault line. I stayed out of the zone, didn't really have an opinion on whether Angel should run off to the convent. And anyways, I was grappling with my own growing desires. Father was deeply religious, though how he rationalized that with his tortured sexual pursuits, I didn't yet know. It would be great to have a nun in the family, he argued. If it didn't work, maybe the sisters would beat some of the rebel out of Angel.

'Who are we to stand in the way of God's plans?' he told Mother one Sunday after dinner. We had been dispatched to our rooms and they glared across the leftover roast beef and mashed potatoes. Father always bellowed authoritatively, spoke ex cathedra, Mother used to say. She thought it would be the ruin of Angel; a reluctant convert, Mother never learned to trust the Roman Catholic clergy.

She blew her nose into the damp handkerchief she kept up her sleeve, fixed her grey eyes on Father's bloodshot baby blues and shouted across the old kitchen table, 'Don't give that girl up to the bloody church!'

That summer Angel went to talk to Father Anthony on Sunday afternoons after Benediction. You could see them through the rectory window, Father Anthony leaning in to scoop up chocolate biscuits the housekeeper placed on the chipped china, Angel holding the teacup the way Mother taught her. All through that July and August, Angel read books Father Anthony had given her and knelt at her bedside late into the night. She also seemed to grow close to Father Anthony.

Angela

This is the last time I send it back to you. You stopped talking years ago. Why are you making trouble now?

Barb

Barb spent the summer volunteering at the rectory, answering the telephone during the hot, sticky evenings. She started going to Mass during the week and spent more time at the tennis courts. Home was strewn with landmines. I stayed out of it, though I wish hadn't. I might have been able to put an end to it. An altar boy like myself sees things, hears things. But I was just too torn apart by my competing desires of spending time on and off the courts with a skinny blonde tennis player named Julie and what I figured was my ticket out of the family – St. Francis Minor Seminary. Angel would glare as Barb teased her blonde hair and showered it with sickly sweet hairspray before heading off to Benediction. Mother and Father tiptoed around the two girls.

Barb

I know you feel hurt about what happened years ago, but stop this. I have enough on my plate.

Angela

They were doing the dishes when it came to a head, Angel splashing lemon suds all over the new kitchen linoleum, her tongue sharp as razors.

'Stop mooning after Father Anthony, for God's sake. He's almost as old as Father. He took a vow: no girlfriends, no wives, no S-E-X. He's not your type . . . He's deep and serious. He doesn't care about your silly crush.'

Barb turned red as sunburn then ran upstairs to her bedroom, slamming the door a mere second ahead of the dam bursting.

Angela:

Typical! You are the only one to have concerns. Just like in your priest days.

Barb

At the end of the summer, Angel went away on retreat north of the city with a group of girls who were thinking about becoming nuns. We're not sure what happened when she was cloistered in those holy woods, but afterwards, Angel never talked about being a nun again. She no longer spent long hours conversing with Father Anthony, who had led the retreat.

Barb meanwhile seemed to have captured Father Anthony's attention. She played tennis with him over the autumn, and asked for special religious instruction.

'What the hell is special religious instruction?' Angel demanded one night when we had crowded around her tiny transistor radio listening to the Beatles.

I'd stayed out of it long enough. I couldn't stand the tension in the house, with my sisters at each other's throats day and night and Mother and Father barely able to speak about it. There were whiffs of rumours about Father Anthony that all the altar boys knew, but up until now I had never said a word at home. The time had come.

'Listen,' I said. 'You two have to stop this. Father Anthony isn't interested in girls.'

Then I stomped out of the room and left them alone with the Beatles.

By Christmas Father Anthony had left the parish. He ran away with Mrs Crozier, the church secretary. The Croziers lived a few blocks from us in a run-down house, had three children; he worked at the racetrack; she wore red lipstick and short skirts, even during Lent. We never saw Father Anthony or Mrs Crozier again.

Angel became preoccupied with the captain of our tennis team. Barb locked herself in her room.

Mother said, 'What would you expect a normal man would do?' then stuck her nose back in her book, curling up in her favourite old armchair. Father said it must have been because Mrs Crozier was from Quebec.

'They can't live without it.'

I was beginning to think I must be part Quebecer.

Angela:

Now I have two of these bleeding things. They are going into the bin. That's where you and I went ages ago.

Barb

Angel and Barb blamed each other for Father Anthony's departure, each figuring the other drove Father Anthony into the arms of the church secretary. They negotiated the confines of our cramped wartime home with diplomatic dexterity, never speaking and rarely looking at one another. Angel moved into the basement and set up her own small bedroom next to the furnace room. The noise drove her into the arms of the first lad who asked her to hitchhike to Vancouver, a lanky Protestant with stubble on his pink cheeks. The ill-fated trip was the beginning of a complicated journey that eventually brought her here to London. She works for the mayor's rent-a-bike scheme. Her partner of five years has just left her for the Irish woman who's been cutting his greying hair for the past year, and she has just found a lump in her breast.

Barb is the head teacher in one of London's academies, making as much as the prime minister, and courting the moneyed classes to keep the academy going. She lives with her husband, a retired Anglican canon she met while on vacation years ago. After decades of fighting women priests, he sits staring out the back window at the cemetery across the road. Barb brings him tea between budget meetings and parent consultations. She has a man friend she visits, an atheist who writes poetry for obscure journals. She never talks about him.

I try not to judge either of them. I've had my own tortured journeys. Alice and I had separated a couple of times but were back together at the end, she being forgiving. What went on between Barb and Angel was a silly sisters' tiff over an unavailable man forty years ago. It makes even less sense today. Still, somehow I blame myself.

Dear Angel and Barb:

I sent you both the posters, hoping to bring you back together after all these years. Sorry. Let me give it one more shot. Come for tea a week Wednesday. I want to see you both, and I have some news to share.

Jackson

There's no sign of them but I haven't given up hope. Call me mad, it's too late for me to care. This has gone on too long and I don't know how much time I have. I've made a salad – lettuce, tomatoes, mushrooms and peppers – and bought some thick-sliced ham from my butcher. There's red and white wine, fruit and some of that black cherry ice cream we used to love as kids. I'm getting sentimental again. It's been worse since Alice passed a year ago with that damned cancer. Maybe it's the medication. The doctor tells me that if I take it faithfully I could have a little longer, but . . .

Is that someone at the door?

The Empty Pew

Scar's pew is empty.

Something's wrong.

If there's one thing that keeps me coming back to the Barracks it's knowing Scar will be sitting on the red-cushioned bench near the gents' at the back of the pub. No one else ever sits in his place. I see him there and know at least something's right in the world.

Tonight, Scar's pew is empty.

I quaff a nervous pint and leave.

A week later I'm back. Still no Scar. He's always here. Something's desperately wrong.

Faye behind the bar, with the streak of blonde hair emanating from dark roots and the England rose tattooed on her propped-up left breast, hasn't had time to think about it today, with the Sunday-night quiz about to start and the lot from Deptford, shaved heads and pony tails, nudging the locals from their pews with dagger eyes. I go looking for Postie. He stops by every day for a 'quick six', knows everybody, every street, close and laneway for a mile around the Barracks, like that guy in the old country song. Postie's not around. Young Bob thinks he knows where Scar rents a room and will check it out. Bob's in the garden shelter, smokers' purgatory. He used to be a porter at the hospital but got sacked for blowing the whistle on his boss taking patients' wagers to the betting shop for a healthy fee. Scar was a good ear for him when that happened. He gets up to go, stubbing his cigarette as he heads through the pub to the front door. Faye will let me know if Scar shows up, and will alert Postie. Heading out the door, I realize I never got around to drinking my pint.

Scar gets his name thanks to the long thin wound that stretches down two inches from the corner of his right eye. Early on, when Scar used to chat more, he told how years ago he got in a fracas with a girl outside the Irish bar in the village, and her boyfriend, a big bearded bloke who rode a motorbike, took a knife to him, sliced him, just missing his eye. The girl ran off. The biker sped away. Scar wouldn't go to the police because he knew he started it. Took a few stitches at the A&E and went home. He never talked about it much. Folks around the pub have heard different versions of the story over the years but that's the one I hold on to. Scar simply found himself in a bad place at a bad time. Got a scar in the process. We've all got them. I don't mind much what the story really is and neither do most of the other regulars, who hold a particular kind of affection for Scar, maybe because of the mysteries around him or possibly just because he's always there. He's a fixture. More than that, though, he doesn't say much, especially these days, he's the one regular who talks to everyone at the Barracks: the quizzers, the Tuesday-night grizzlies, the Friday-night party folks, the late-night gents, the post-match red-scarfed Addicks back from another loss at the Valley, and the so-called intellectuals in their linen jackets closeted in the dark corner at the front of the pub.

When I first encountered Scar we had a few conversations about family – mine, not his – and he always checked with me on how Charlton Athletic were doing as the season unfolded. I used to marvel at how drinkers from every corner would nonchalantly make their way over to his pew one at a time, get a few words, a handshake, a laugh and then move on. Everyone got to know him a little. He got to know a lot about the folks who frequent the Barracks.

Over the years, Scar has withdrawn a bit. He still says 'hi' to everyone but the conversations are brief, muted. He's changed in other ways too. The stubble on Scar's face has grown thicker and greyer as the stubble on top of his oversized head has been reduced to peach fuzz. These days his eyelids droop and I wonder if that's why he always seems to be looking down towards his newspaper. In the past few months his face has looked swollen as if he is on some kind of meds. I try talking to him about it and he just mutters towards his crossword.

'Fine, thanks. You take care.'

Scar always has a pint of lager in front of him, whether he buys it or someone brings one over. That happens a lot. People feel comfortable with him there. He always asks how you're doing, no matter who you are, fixes you with a quizzical gaze, chats in monosyllables about the races or football then ends the conversation abruptly, putting his pencil to work again on the newspaper. You learn to move on. Lately, Scar's been mixing his drinks, taking a cider one round then some of the cheap red wine they sell at the Barracks and adding ice for some godforsaken reason. Ask Scar about that and he grows a deaf ear.

I mostly huddle in a corner on one of the curved benches – pews they call them here, God knows why. If I wanted pews I'd cross the road to the old church. I came to the Barracks soon after arriving from Canada a half dozen years ago. I can never tell if it's the best mock-English pub or the best authentic one, with its dark redwood walls, English knick-knacks, photos of telly comics I've never heard of and ragged paperbacks amid the cloistered clutter. But it's a comfortable old pub. Like a lot of folks, I've made it my second home. There are two ways of attending the Barracks. Get yourself a pint of lager and a packet of salted peanuts, find a quiet corner, open your newspaper and ignore the argy-bargy, maybe keep an eye on the front door in case someone you want to talk to shows. Or, gather in one of the circles of folks on cushioned pews, mini-armchairs and stools around the tiny pockmarked tables with packets of crisps, pints and wine glasses competing for space, and chip in on the local gossip.

Scar is always there, part of the crowd, inhaling the beery Barracks atmosphere, but is somehow on his own. Maybe you go there first for the anonymity, but things change quickly enough. You soon get caught up in a kind of church life, or, as the linen-jacket corner would have it, *community*. Scar is different. He's in the crowd, connected even, but on his own.

I'm not sure when Scar first came to the Barracks. It was a long time before I showed up, maybe twenty-five years ago. And I'm not certain what drew him to the pub and kept him there. He always comes alone and I've never heard of a wife, girlfriend or kids. I just know that he's not in his pew again. Folks say Scar came from the coast but I've never heard which city, and they said he came alone. I've heard stories about how he used to make his living writing gags for BBC radio, worked on small newspapers as a cartoonist and ended up in the jewellery-making world before he got sacked for taking too much of an interest in the boss's daughter. If you put it all together, it's quite a CV. But it's hard to know what part of it is truth and what part of it is fiction, and Scar just laughs off questions about the past.

These days only the odd Barracks newcomer ever asks where he's from or what kind of work or family stories he wants to share, but Scar gives them his characteristic stare and then shakes his head as he lowers it to the ever-present newspaper on his lap. Or, he turns it back to them. 'Never mind that, tell me how the kids in America are? Is your wife over that flu?'

Folks have learned to keep some distance on Scar's past, but of course Scar's not the only one with a past. In one of my earliest conversations with Scar, he asked about my ex-wife back home and offered a sweaty old hand on my back as I laid it all bare (or most of it), perhaps after one too many pints. Actually, now that I think about it, it was most certainly after far too many pints. Those were the days. Scar never raised it again.

The next day I find Postie at the bar with his eye on the door like he's expecting someone to come through any moment. I oblige. His brow is all furrowed so I know he's worried. He says Bob never found Scar. He knocked on the door of the house where he thought Scar had a room and they'd never heard of him. They didn't speak English but Bob got the point. Scar didn't live there. Postie says we should get a group together and go looking for Scar. A couple of pints later we have a plan. We will meet at the Barracks at the end of Postie's shift the next day, break into groups and scour the square mile around the pub. Bob will phone some of the regulars that went on the Medway cruise a while back. Postie will map out several routes for the volunteers. I'll talk to the police officer I know in the village, see if he can help us. He's been to the Barracks once or twice and remembers who Scar is. Faye's been on the phone to the hospital but they have no record of him being admitted. She'll make a poster to publicize the search. She's got a fuzzy photo of Scar on her phone taken at the barbecue last year. I buy her a pint and she gives me her 'you're a dirty old man' scowl. I finish my lager and head home. I'm tired, haven't been sleeping so well lately.

Postie is what the lads at the Valley call a 'unit', six-foot four, and in his yellow rain gear he looks like a solid line down the middle of a carriageway. He's standing outside the Barracks when I arrive. Under his hood I can see the shadowed rows of his forehead. He wants to know where the hell I've been, glances at his watch. He's part worried about Scar and part excited about something. He pushes his head towards the door of the Barracks like Big Mak at the Valley poking one into the goal from a corner (as if that ever actually happens), muttering for me to look in. It's hazy in there, not like in the smoking days, but with steam coming off all the wellies and raincoats of two dozen Barracks regulars set to go searching for Scar. Jesus. My eyes go damp for a second but it's probably just from the rain.

'We've got a regular posse in there,' I offer.

Postie's got a map of the area he thinks we should search and he lays it on the bar after Faye moves a few coasters and glasses out of the way. It's a rough kind of inverted triangle with the Barracks at the bottom, the posh homes running up the left-hand side and the council homes and one block of private flats running up the right. Lots of green space in between. At the Barracks you often don't at first know if you're sharing elbow space with a retired banker or the guy who delivers the pizza adverts through your letter box. Scar talks to them all and a fair bunch of them have showed up to try and find him today. Postie splits us into four groups, one headed to the council flats, another to the posh road, the third to the old church, football pitch and graveyard. The fourth group he takes charge of himself, leading us beyond the triangle through a network of laneways and alleys I never knew existed. The police man joins us in his jeans and green rain gear and we follow Postie and the tall American engineer, apparently one of the last Barracks regulars to have spoken with Scar a couple of weeks ago, though I have no idea what they chatted about. A dark-haired woman in her forties, who's wearing hiking boots and a grim demeanour, peers into every crevice, rubbish bin and fence hole we pass like she's done this before. Someone says she knew Scar back in the day, whatever that means. I've never seen her at the Barracks before.

No one says much as we trail down the alleys ripe with dog shit and fox piss and wet leaves that we kick away cautiously in case we find something underneath. Postie checks his phone every few minutes but says nothing. We wander for more than an hour when the American says he's thirsty and could really use a pint. He's not optimistic about the search, I'd say. He's probably not the only one. Postie grimaces but I think it's as much because we can't find any trace of Scar. He nudges us back toward the Barracks. As we retrace our steps, we stick our heads over unpainted fences and push at garage doors to see if they budge as we go, then trudge towards the pub for a pint. Faye says the landlady is buying the first one for the searchers. We get a couple of pints each and sit near the back of the pub across from Scar's pew. No one looks over. Somebody buys peanuts and crisps and splits the bags open for everyone to lean in and grab a few. I'm suddenly hungry and thirsty. I take a long draught of my lager and things start to feel almost normal, except we didn't find Scar. Neither did any of the other groups.

Postie is up and down for the next hour as he checks with the searchers as they come back to the Barracks. He doesn't say anything when we quiz him as he sits back down, just shakes his head. Nothing. After a couple more pints, the lads quietly get up and leave, drifting out the door in twos or threes. Soon there's just Postie, Bob and me, and Faye behind the bar. She keeps wiping her eyes on her sleeve. Postie tries to buy her a drink and she tells him to piss off. We leave by the side door, nodding without a word.

We're not on Postie's route so I'm gobsmacked when I see him coming to our front door next morning. We're only an eight-minute walk from the Barracks. Postie's been here once before for a Christmas do. He didn't leave until nearly sunlight. He's been a good friend ever since. Today the kettle's hissing so I can make myself a cup of tea; those pints last night are taking their toll. I rub some of the night from my eyes. Postie looks like shit, stooped over like I've never seen him before, eyes red. As soon as I open the door, I know it's about Scar. He looks down at his boots, says Faye called him because the Met came to the Barracks when she was opening up, said they found a body down by the river, way beyond our little triangle. Kids riding their bikes just about ran over him as they were chasing each other. Christ. They're pretty sure it's Scar but they want Postie and someone else from the pub to have a look.

Of course it's Scar. Maybe someday I'll talk about what we saw down by the river but I doubt it. My wife didn't ask for any details. Thank God. She's good that way. Let's just say it wasn't pretty and it was no way for a likeable bloke like Scar to end up, or any of us, for that matter. The Met say there was no knifing, no suicide. Looks like Scar just went to die by the river. Didn't want a fuss, I guess. He's been there a few days in some brush they hadn't cut due to the rain. Postie and I needed a few pints after that, though there wasn't much conversation, just a lot of head shaking and some serious cursing as it sank in. Scar is gone for good. Shit.

At noon a week later the Barracks is packed. The Tuesday-night grizzlies, the Friday-night crowd, even a few quizzers from Deptford, are there. Faye's behind the bar with the landlady and her skinny teenaged son. Faye has dark bags under her eyes, like she forgot her makeup. Nobody's drinking. It's dead quiet and barrel-chested Lewis stands on a chair. It's a bit dodgy so the grim woman from the search steadies it. Lewis points over to Scar's pew. There's a print of that fuzzy photo of Scar and a red rose on the table. It must have been Faye who did that. Scar loaned her some money once when her boyfriend left her and she couldn't make the rent, the same lad I saw Scar trying to talk some sense into soon afterwards. Scar had his arm around his shoulder and was real animated. The young man looked dazed – by drink or drugs or the worldly wisdom of Scar, I don't really know. But the scene stayed with me like an old movie that keeps playing in your head long after you've watched it.

Lewis has known Scar longer than anybody, maybe even from their days on the coast before coming to the big city. He clears his throat, thanks the landlady for hosting the *memorial*, though he mangles the word like he wasn't expecting to have to say it. Lewis has done this kind of thing before but Scar's been part of his life for a long time. The thing about Scar, he says, is how he never made a single enemy in the Barracks in all his years of coming in for a pint. He may have made some mistakes in the past, but he always treated folks at the Barracks well, talked to everybody, even if it was just to see how they were doing. He never got involved in any of the groups in the pub or the controversies about the loud music or the debate about the protests when the government tried to close the hospital. There were lots of different views about those things and around the Europe referendum among folks at the pub and sometimes the Barracks tribe was sorely tested. But Scar chatted a bit to everyone, Lewis says. Heads nod around the room, a few smiles break out too as folks remember the most recent General Election and the time the former MP brought some party literature into the Barracks and the landlady had to walk the retired politician to the door, handing him back his fat wad of flyers. Apparently Scar had a good old quiet laugh about that back in his corner.

Now the American engineer pushes his way in the side door, late. Folks say he hates funerals so it's saying something he's here at all. Postie looks at the ceiling. I don't see young Bob and wonder if he showed. Lewis takes out his handkerchief and gives it a long hard blow. He looks like an old sea captain and when he blows his nose it sounds like he's clearing the harbour for his freight. There is a long silence and then he continues.

'That's what Scar did,' Lewis says. 'He helped keep us talking to each other.'

There's dead silence for a few moments. Lewis is about to

say more but first gets his handkerchief out again. So the landlady rings the bell. The memorial is over, she declares, her damp eyes offering a gesture of thanks to Lewis. The first round's on her, she says.

Some folks leave right away but most get a pint. I hang around a bit, sitting in one of the few quiet corners with my lager, ignoring the growing clamour all around me. Postie comes over and I just wave him away. He knows me well enough to leave me in my solitary corner among the used paperbacks and beer magazines. People are mingling about, not sure what to say, letting the beer take its course. The engineer is telling Faye about the last conversation he had with Scar. Postie is now dodging questions about us going to identify Scar. I can't really taste my lager and I'm not sure I want to be here. Worse, I'm not sure what to think about Scar. It's like we knew him so well and yet not at all. There are so many gaps in his story. I take a sip of the lager but it doesn't taste right. And I wonder what the Barracks will be like now that Scar is gone.

The Barracks is starting to get noisy now, the mourners becoming partiers as the alcohol hits them. I'm not ready for that yet. I get up and piss off out the door without saying 'cheerio' to anyone to find my way home. On the way up the gloomy side street I catch a glimpse of my own battered face in the window of the landlady's new SUV and have to wonder what the hell kind of battle folks looking out their windows will think I've been through.

For weeks now I've been coming into the Barracks and the photo and shrivelled rose sit on Scar's pew. Some folks have been giving it a lift of their glass before wandering to their corner or out into smokers' purgatory. But that's happening less and less as time goes by.

Today I arrive at the Barracks looking for a pint of lager and glance down the bar and see a newcomer sitting in Scar's pew, of all the bloody things! Of course, he looks friendly enough, but that's hardly the point. I feel my face start burning and turn in his direction when Faye takes my paltry bit of change and smacks it smartly on the bar, freezing me with her glare.

'Scar's gone, mate,' she says.

Of course, he is. Of course, he is.

I take my beer to a corner and muscle down a long bitter gulp, open my packet of salted peanuts and check the back pages of the newspaper.

Harmony

I head to the pub, hoping to catch up with Ger. Moira has gone home now and he'll have some gossip about her. We'll talk football and the news, take the piss over a pint.

When I come out of my house, my neighbour is working in her garden. She's stooped over but stands up straight and gives me her familiar wave. She knows where I am headed. She smiles under that ridiculous gardening hat, brushes her eye with her worn right glove then bends back towards her greenery. My neighbour's garden is coming along.

*

It was the day our next-door neighbour Stanley stumbled down the stairs of his newly renovated townhouse and broke his neck that I realized my marriage of twenty years was over.

Stanley was regal, tall with bushy white eyebrows and long curly greying hair. He carried himself like a man who held power and wielded it ruthlessly yet was able to carry it off with an air of grace. He approached his house every afternoon at 5:55 p.m. from the university where he taught English Literature to students from around the world, looking neither left nor right, and with the urgency of a royal who knew that his tea was on his oak dining-room table and his faithful wife ready to attend.

But Stanley lived alone.

Despite his air of indestructibility, with his height of well over six foot three inches and his elegant gait that poked his rather handsome and distinguished beak towards the heavens, we came to know him as quite dependent over the decade he lived beside us in our modest close near the royal park.

However, his dependence was focused solely on my wife, Sal, who is the kind of woman who takes neighbourliness seriously.

I only discovered just how close they were when Stanley slipped on the top step of his townhouse stairs while moving the contents of his ancient desk drawer upstairs after the workmen had taken the desk itself back up. Sal heard the loud crash and rushed over immediately and phoned an ambulance – but it was too late. When I arrived home from our local a half-hour later, the close was a riot of flashing blue lights, and Sal was inside Stanley's doorway on her hands and knees wiping up his black blood like it was crude oil from a leaky tanker.

'He's dead,' she whispered, like it was a secret, though by then it was pretty clear to me, with the ambulance and police cars littered around our close – and the blood. Sal's face alone would have told me, too, twisted out of shape like she had just been sick to her stomach. I started picking up the papers strewn at the bottom of the stairs and Sal suggested I take them next door to ours and organize them. Outside, the neighbours were still gathering despite the late hour and were sorting out how to reach Stanley's elderly cousin somewhere in the Middle East. I nodded to Strudwick, our nearest neighbour on the other side. He was holding his wife, Marta, who had tears streaming down her cheeks. Strudwick was silent, just stood shaking his head gravely. They weren't close to Stanley but they always tried to talk with him if they ran into him in the village. Stanley seemed to think he was above them somehow, perhaps because they worked in television. Stanley didn't own one. A couple of other neighbours, Alfie, who I had chatted with earlier at the pub a few streets away, and some new folks I didn't know well, just looked at their feet as the ambulance prepared to carry Stanley away to the local hospital morgue. I headed straight to our door.

The papers amounted to mostly bills promptly paid, receipts for books from New York and Berlin and a few scattered thank-you notes from colleagues at the university, and I arranged them into piles and then found envelopes from my own dusty desk to put them in some kind of order. There were also two notes in pink envelopes marked with the simple salutation 'Stanley' on the outside. Something about the handwriting made me curious and I opened one.

*

Our close sits on the edge of this east-end village, an hour from the city, a little haven of hospitality in the midst of the metropolis, sometimes fictional, sometimes real. There are restaurants, pubs, too many estate agents, but it's the kind of small community where you were bound to bump into a neighbour anytime you were rushing to the train station or wandering to the park. Our close, Harmony Close (we sometimes laughed about that), is a reflection of the village, at times tight-knit, other times gossipy and snarly, depending on what kind of issues were being dealt with at the annual meetings of the residents' association – tree cutting, spraying the weeds with poisons, parking problems. Those kinds of things can bring you together – or drive you apart. In the time we have lived here, Sal has made herself indispensable. If there was a letter to be written, a sick neighbour to be visited, a cake to be baked, Sal was front of the queue.

Stanley had lived in the house next door as long as anyone could remember. Apparently, in the early days here he brought home a young woman, brown haired, with freckles and a curious walk that made her resemble an awkward giraffe. Neighbours thought it must have been his wife joining him from overseas, but she rarely appeared in the village and after a few months just disappeared. Nothing more was said of her but then Stanley never said much anyways.

Sal was probably one of the only ones Stanley talked to. She was approachable, always up for a wee chat and didn't go in for the vicious rumours, and she'd do anything for you.

A few years ago Stanley twisted his ankle on the icy walkway at the university and came home in a black cab much later than usual, and Sal, who was arriving from stacking shelves at the local library, helped him into his house, poured him a cup of tea and then made him beans on toast, something Stanley said he had never actually eaten before. We had a good little laugh at home about that. Over the next couple of weeks, Sal was over at Stanley's as much as she was at home.

I went off to the pub for a pint. The last thing I would have thought was that Sal was seeing too much of Stanley. Pompous, he was. But harmless, surely.

*

Harmony Close is your utilitarian L-shaped little enclave, with box-shaped townhouses inhabited by a more intimate version of the wider city, with various kinds of families, ethnic origins and levels of friendliness and grouchiness. Lately it has seen more renters move in as original owners pass away and their offspring decide to hang on to a well-placed bit of real estate or as retirees take extended trips to Berlin or Vancouver. So it sometimes takes a little more to keep the communal activities going, like the Christmas party Sal organizes every year at our place, offering those puffy little savoury nibbles from the delicatessen in the village and the bottles of red and white wine we sometimes buy at the wine shop near the old Roman Catholic church by the heath. Or if there is a special occasion like the bonfire or the Big Lunch, she is at the heart of the organizing, knocking on doors or sending emails to try and get volunteers.

'It's important and nobody else is going to do it so I just like to get it started,' she says. Strudwick and his wife Marta have been corralled a few times, and I sometimes think they keep their eyes down when they see her coming in the village, lest she have another project in mind.

*

Stanley's relatives didn't really want a big funeral so Sal invited them and all the neighbours in the close for a couple of hours on a Friday night for a quiet glass of wine and dainty bits of foreign cheese. We lit some candles and Stanley's ancient cousin said a few words. He mumbled a bit, but I think I made out that Stanley may not have had many friends or close relatives; however, he truly loved his books. Marta asked me later if any students had been invited, but Sal had found the school somewhat uncooperative when she was trying to organize the wake. Most of our close neighbours were there, though they didn't say a lot and left after just one glass of wine. Sonny from across the road spilled his Merlot on the white living room wall he was leaning on and spent most of the wake trying to wipe it down with his handkerchief. Sal just shook her head and went on taking care of everyone like it never happened.

The next morning at breakfast, I put the papers from Stanley's drawer on the kitchen counter to show Sal before the cousin came by to pick them up. The two pink envelopes in her perfect script were on top. She just looked at me – then burst into tears.

*

I loathe flying, and a long flight to the upside-down part of the planet is torture. But this time I didn't give a damn. I strapped in for the first of three flights that would take me to Wellington in New Zealand. Ger, my mate from the pub, had a friend who had a cottage on Raumati Beach, an hour north of Wellington. He looked at the state of me over a dark pint and basically ordered me out of the country. On the plane I hooked up my earphones and watched mindless film after mindless film, and only in the final hours of the final flight did I begin to understand that my marriage was over and that my life would never be the same again. I tried crying but the tears wouldn't come, and so I closed my eyes and dreamed half-awake of the sweet early days with Sal, when we were both working so hard, me at the betting shop and her at the library, yet we found a way to cherish our time together – picnics on the big old bed we had before it literally fell apart beneath us, and all night bingeing on the early version of what we now call box sets.

The Kiwi friend of my mate Ger met me at the airport. Moira was a large brassy artist who owned a string of small galleries on the North Island. She was all smiles and bangles of wood jewellery that you could hear a mile away, and she wore the scent of an old lover from before my marriage. She must have known my story because she was also full of generous nods and headshaking as she listened to me prattle on during the hour-long drive north along the rain-soaked Kapiti coastline. She dropped me off at her rough old beach house, a white cabin sitting on a hill just a few yards from the sea, showed me how to turn on the water and where to find blankets and took me around the corner to the nearest little grocery shop run by a family of quiet smiling Indians. Then she was gone. If circumstances had been different I'm sure we would have had a great chat and gossiped a bit about our mutual mate. But I was glad to be left on my own.

After getting some basic food from the store, I went back to the beach house, made myself a cheese sandwich and collapsed in the rickety old bed, leaving my tea on the locker beside the bed to go cold. I slept for nearly twelve hours straight.

When I woke up, the sun was setting across the ocean and I went outside and sat on the wooden deck chair amid the huge white cotton clouds pressed against the reddening sky, and finally wept like a baby.

*

When Sal stopped crying she began her part of the story.

I know this won't sound right because it's the kind of story I've heard or read or watched in movie theatres a thousand times. Somehow we just got too comfortable with one another; somehow she felt I didn't need her anymore; somehow Stanley was there at the right time; somehow she needed his need.

Beyond that, Sal didn't say much. It began slowly; sex wasn't the biggest part of it; he was a lovely man; much misunderstood; we never wanted to hurt you; he's gone now, can't we start again; she still loved me.

I think I just said one word. 'No.'

There wasn't much more to add. She was weeping with her face in her hands so I could barely make out the words, but I got the message. Good thing we were seated at a solid quartz countertop in our renovated kitchen or I would have picked up the table and thrown it at the wall. I walked out the front door, slamming it shut so loudly that Strudwick stuck his head out his front window then looked away again when he saw the state of me, a raging Lear threatening the clouds. I walked back into the house an hour later, after huffing around the park, to get my wallet, then stole out again to the pub. Sal was still on her kitchen stool, her head in her hands, but there was no sound from her. Maybe her crying, at least, was over. Mine hadn't yet begun.

*

If you descend the half dozen steps from the beach house to the sea front you enter another realm. My pub mate Ger had warned me back home to bring ear plugs because the roar of the sea is constant, but I needed that roar those first few hours of walking the beach, crunching barefoot along the floor of silt, sand and a rainbow of damp sea shells. I walked at the beginning of the day or at the end so saw few of my neighbours. It was cool and windy, out of season, though there was the odd dog walker and a few silent fishermen waiting for a tug on their lines as they scanned the horizon. The sea was rough and relentless and the sky wild and without end. Everything out of doors on those long daily walks became minuscule in comparison. It helped me first to not think – but soon enough to think a hell of a lot.

I needed to purge – and purge I did. I cursed Stanley and his pomposity, Sal and her bloody-minded naiveté, the world for its lack of fairness. And I cursed myself for letting it all happen, spending too much time at the pub, too much time just ignoring the daily details of domestic life, too much time taking it all for granted: Sal, the marriage, the sweet complacent life of no real worry or engagement. Sal somehow fell for Stanley – but it was as if I stood there watching it all unfold like I was at the movies, frozen in my comfortable balcony seat, popcorn in hand, and couldn't really do anything about it. The sea made me forget one moment, and remember the next. It was dark, foreboding, relentless, unforgiving.

When I wasn't walking the sea shore I rode the local bus, partly just to keep occupied and learn something of my local neighbourhood. But it also took me to the library and the internet, a larger grocery store and a bookstore, all dangerous for their own reasons. The B4 went right by my temporary home, invisible from the street because it was down a long driveway, then circled back past it again. I always seemed to mess up the schedule and get there at the wrong time, which meant a half-hour wait. I'd sit down on the kerb to think. Locals walking past gave me confused looks but never said much. New Zealanders were polite. On the B4, older women and young mums and their children in too-wide buggies clambered on and off all the way to the library. They all seemed to know each other and the driver, swapped photos back and forth of their grandchildren and cousins living in Australia or America. I never experienced that back home. I wondered if that kind of conversation continued once they got to their streets. Was there a Sal in their close? A Stanley? I got off the bus at the library and checked my email. Another message from Sal awaited, but again I didn't open it.

*

Moira came by the beach house, the old-lover scent blowing in with the sea breeze, her wooden beads jangling like those of the ancient friars I used to know. We made tea and sat on the simple wooden deck in hard chairs staring out at the ocean, watching the cloud formations change like it was television stations, one moment it was a ship heading across the sky, the next a grey-bearded god from some holy scripture.

She didn't say much for a while, then gave me a curious look, then spoke. 'Have you heard from Sal?'

'No.'

'But Ger said she was trying to reach you.'

'Possibly, but I don't have email here, do I?'

'You can get thirty minutes free at the library.'

'I know that. I was there today but didn't see anything from her,' I lied.

Her scowl said she didn't believe me.

We moved on to wine. White for her, red for me.

Not a good idea.

I brought out some crisps I had bought at the grocery store and we dug in, licking the salt off our fingers, laughing softly about that as we somehow did it in tandem. The crisps sent us after more wine. The red was working on me. I felt lighter, as if I didn't have a care in the world, as if the news of a fling in New Zealand, a million miles away from Sal and Harmony Close didn't matter a fig. I got up to use the loo but when I came back Moira was nowhere to be seen, though the scent of her hung on the bushes next to the ancient table, now pockmarked with red wine stains.

Just as well.

*

After a month, I'd had enough. It was the kind of place I would have spent six months with Sal. She would have loved the little social club around the corner from the bus stop, where the sweet young waiter with the ring in his nose made such a fuss over man and woman alike and just plain made everyone feel welcome; the fish was local and delicious, the beer local and passable; there was jazz on a Friday night if you booked ahead. It would have been a real treat, the whole scene, if Sal had been part of the picture. Now, I just needed to get back and figure out what my life was going to be about.

On board I got stuck between two big business blokes from Australia and buried myself in Katharine Mansfield stories so as not to have to talk to them. It was a long bloody journey without much chance to stretch my legs, and when I got back home I took a cab to Harmony Close. I tried not to look at Stanley's house, though I could see that it had been painted and the front garden tidied up. Ger was waiting there with my post and some advice. I was knackered and wasn't much in the mood for listening.

'You need to read those emails from Sal.'

'All in good time.'

'Look, things have changed . . .'

'No shit.'

'I mean beyond the obvious.'

'Well, you're dying to tell me, so why don't you just go ahead and do it.'

'It's better you read the emails.'

'Whatever you say, Ger.'

But I didn't. I went grocery shopping, stocked up on wine in the village shop Sal always said was too expensive, sent a card off to Moira in New Zealand and started going through the house, room by room, to see where I needed to begin cleaning. Every piece of furniture was in the same place as before but the house had somehow changed. Sal had said before I left that she would just pack up her clothes and a few personal things and leave. I had no doubt that was exactly what she did, but the house had altered dramatically though I couldn't put my finger on what was different. Before starting the clean-up, I put the kettle on and searched for the least dusty cup, when the doorbell rang. I ignored it. It rang again. I ignored it. Again. Next thing I knew, I could hear the door being unlocked. I turned around and Sal was standing in front of me.

*

The first time I met Sal was twenty-five years ago when she came into the betting shop with her husband, a brown-haired shy young man who wanted to place his first bet on a horse at the Grand National. She came along for moral support and I got chatting with her while he went over the race listings. After he placed his bet they left, but she came back a few minutes later and handed me a piece of paper. I thought it was another bet and said I would be right with her but she disappeared and I was left holding a lined bit of notepad with her name and phone number on it, her distinctive handwriting glanced for the first time. A few days later I called. At first we met for brief chats over tea on the outskirts of the village or hiked down past the park to the movie house to watch the foreign films she liked. Every now and then I would tempt her to my house in the close that my old aunt had left me when I first got out of school, and we would play at being husband and wife in my rickety old bed, make tea and grilled cheese sandwiches, then she would run off home before her husband got back from football or a night out drinking with his mates. She always said he was more interested in that life than in being a husband.

After a year of this sneaking around, she left him and moved in with me. When she got her divorce six months later, we got married at the registry office, just us and a few friends attending. But it was the beginning of a long, good spell. I remember her face that first day in the betting shop, beautiful without the makeup most of her friends were wearing, part innocence and part flirtation. Sal was always full of both invitation and threat, so open-minded you couldn't help but be pulled into her world, though you soon realized you were in for far more than you expected. Early on she would invite me to go for a walk along the river and I'd agree but soon find myself in a five-hour hike in the pouring rain, culminating in a trip to the best hiking store downtown to buy hundreds of pounds' worth of boots, poles and hiking clothes that we might never use again. This sort of thing happened all the time, and while I never quite learned to say 'no' to her, I did develop a healthy caution when I agreed to her latest adventure. She would give that commanding look of innocent flirtation and off we would go.

*

So there it was again, that look that told me she, or perhaps we, were somehow about to embark on a new adventure. How the hell could that be true? Of course, I should have opened her emails. I should have listened to Ger. I should have done a lot of things, a long time ago. What she told me the day I arrived home from New Zealand didn't so much shock me as turn me upside down. I felt like I was back on Raumati Beach or that I should get on a plane and strap myself in for another long haul, go find Moira and figure out why she had taken off just when there might have been a moment of mad sensation. I decided to just listen, and I did, for a long bloody hour. One of the things I realized as Sal spoke quietly, eloquently, emphatically for that hour, was how seldom I did just that – listen to her. But the words themselves were like a fairy tale without the happy ending, for me at any rate. It was Sal at her best, naiveté, optimism and practical tough love. But it made no sense to me. It just wouldn't work. When she left, I went off to the pub to think it through, hoping I wouldn't run into Ger or anyone else I knew. I just wanted to get pissed.

*

The Big Lunch was almost a year later and Harmony Close made a grand party out of it, partly because so much had gone on over the past year. Sal and I had parted company. Strudwick and his wife had made a television movie that had been well received though it was broadcast late at night and most of us hadn't actually seen it. Alfie across the road had died suddenly of cancer that his doctor had apparently failed to diagnose despite numerous visits to the surgery over the past year. Some new folks had moved into his place and there was a lot of nervousness among the old timers because they were brown skinned and two of the women, mother and daughter, I think, wore veils and didn't talk much to the other women in the close. Things had changed.

I invited Ger and he brought Moira, who was visiting from New Zealand. She gave me a sweet past-lover-scented jangly hug and kiss and went off and helped Strudwick with the barbecue. Ger and I blocked off the close from traffic then blew up some balloons for the kids. The wee ones belonging to the new neighbours across the road slowly made their way from their front garden and grabbed royal-blue balloons from us under the watchful eyes of their parents. It was a grand little event and everyone wanted to talk to Moira about her place in New Zealand, probably because I had bored them with my own stories for the past year.

But the star of the Big Lunch was Sal, still in the close, still looking after everyone's needs, still making sure we weren't just a row of townhouses but some kind of extended family in this mad old city we inhabit. She had been to the wine store and went around to all the families offering red or white, and even got the new neighbours to sit down and have some barbecued chicken and rice, and non-alcoholic wine. I could see it all happening across the road as I sat sipping a beer with Ger. Sal was showing the new folks the ingredients on the bottle of non-wine. She soon had them laughing and sipping, very gingerly, the sparkling liquid in their plastic glasses.

Ger turned to me and asked in his blunt but not unpleasant way: 'So, how's that going, then?'

'God knows,' I said.

'I told you to check your email.' He laughed.

'A lot of good that would have done me.'

He didn't disagree with that.

*

'That', as Ger referred to it, was the fact that Sal had inherited Stanley's house. She now lived next door to me, had no intention of moving and told me she was happy enough if I just stayed. I'd lived most of my life in the close and wasn't about to move and she knew it. If all this sounds odd, it is, frankly. Very odd. Strudwick just shakes his head when he sees Sal running around the close on her missions of mercy, though I know his wife Marta is suspicious of why Sal stayed on and why I didn't move. Most of the other neighbours don't say anything about the situation though I know they are delighted to have Sal here in the close. The Big Lunch was a great success and everyone praised Sal for that.

To be honest, I don't know if I will ever get used to it. It is always tough living cheek to jowl with neighbours in such a close, Harmony or not. But this is a step beyond that. Whether it is a step too far or not, I will find out.

It's like Sal has taken me, and the whole close, on one of those long walks that might turn into a great adventure – or some kind of disaster. I won't deny it scares me but I guess I am still intrigued. Something keeps me in this place with these neighbours – all of them.

*

I head to the pub, hoping to catch up with Ger. Moira has gone home now and he'll have some gossip about her. We'll talk football and the news, take the piss over a pint.

When I come out of my house, my neighbour is working in her garden. She's stooped over but stands up straight and gives me her familiar wave. She knows where I am headed. She smiles under that ridiculous gardening hat, brushes her eye with her worn right glove then bends back towards her greenery. My neighbour's garden is coming along.

A Meeting of Minds

Kenneth winces from the dank stench of piss, sweat and alcohol as he approaches the mound of garish sleeping bag in the polished doorway of the local town hall. Thin and pale with well-manicured hands, the thirty-year-old conference coordinator gently lifts his black leather attaché case over the mound, taking care not to disturb either. The door is locked but there is a light on inside and a burly brown security guard ambles towards the glass entrance, slightly tinted by the morning frost and sweet heat of the mound. Kenneth adjusts his hair, short, black and waxed. He's pleased he wore the grey tie and black jacket. He looks down at his shoes, frowns, and then buffs each against the back of the opposite pant leg. As he is about to enter the now unlocked door, Kenneth, who hasn't had his first jolt of morning coffee yet, turns and whispers hoarsely to the mound. 'I'm so sorry, but you can't stay there. In half an hour we will have some important doctors and health scientists here for a conference. You have to move.'

He then follows the security man in through several sets of doors to the conference hall, trying not to think 'Exhibit A'.

Mac smells the urine too, feels it, tastes it. It is part of him. It must have been the cheap cider. Fuck. But he's not moving. It's awful. It's cold. It stinks. He stinks. His head hurts. Everything hurts. He is freezing and wet. But this is where he sleeps. Usually nobody comes near this door until late afternoon except the dark-eyed receptionist, who sometimes brings him a steaming milky tea. This is his space. This is his home. Even if his body would move, something holds him back. He can't budge. He's not yet sure that he is actually alive. He is carrying this massive weight, more than his grey-bearded bulk.

Half an hour later, Kenneth is standing over the mound. He has put out a sandwich board announcing the speaker: 'Doctor Fischer, Berlin expert on health and the homeless'.

Kenneth speaks rapidly to the mound, his voice now like stretched elastic. 'Listen, our guests will be arriving any minute. I have to ask you to move. Can I … get the security man to help you move around the corner there?'

There is no answer. Mac appears to be asleep.

*

The motor on the small creaking fishing boat stutters through wailing wind, rumbling thunder and lightning that cracks open an electric sky.

Father and son are at sea. Father's voice is distant gravel in the wind.

'Pull the net in, son. We're headin' to shore. It's real bad. Pull the net in. Do you hear me? Pull the net in.'

'I can't, Dad. I can't reach it. I'm gonna fall in. Help me.'

'You ain't gonna fall in. Steady now, reach to your left. Grab that rope. Grab it. Jesus, son. Grab that rope.'

'I can't, Dad. I can't do it. I can't reach.'

Father stretches his lungs to have his voice reach the boy through the wind. 'Bloody hell. Not that one, the other one. You'll put us in the drink … Grab the heavy rope.'

'I'm trying but I can't get it. You have to help. You have to come here …'

'I ain't able to let go o' the wheel, son. I'm stuck here. You'll have to …'

'Is this the one?'

The boy is a whisper in the violent wash of the storm, but Father hears.

'No, not that one. It's the other one. That's the one. Don't lean so far …'

There's a loud splash then a clap of thunder. Father hears neither. The motor stalls.

'Dad, help, help, help, hel—'

'Son, no, no, no.'

*

Mac awakens and sticks his head outside the sleeping bag just in time to puke on the paving stones. He's been moved away from the front of the hall and he sees two men walking away from him as he lifts his head from the pool of vomit. The big man is slouching, the smaller bloke gestures as if his hands are in need of a wash. Mac goes behind the building with his bulging ancient rucksack to piss and change his clothes.

The conference is going well. Kenneth slips outside for a few moments at the lunch break to have a cigarette. He started when he was eleven. All the lads at that place were puffing at that age. There were no mothers or fathers to tell them to quit. And smoking was the least of their troubles. He begins to feel butterflies in his chest, but he catches himself, takes another drag on his cigarette. That was then. He nods and scrunches up his shoulders in response to the half waves from the small circle of suits pinned with plastic nametags.

Out of the corner of his eye he sees a bear of a man sitting on the yellow sleeping bag. His hair is matted with grime but looks like it has been haphazardly combed; his beard is long and straggly. The man is wearing several worn jackets, the top layer brown with an oily stain. He is watching the planes circle over the heath towards Heathrow Airport. There is a plastic bottle beside him nearly drained of cheap clear cider, the kind they sell for a couple of pounds on the high street. The man has moved a few paces back towards the front doors.

Kenneth slowly approaches, holding his cigarette behind him.

'Excuse me. You really need to stay clear of the doorway. As I explained . . .'

'Have you got a cigarette, mate?' Mac asks.

Kenneth brings his hand around in front of him as if he just discovers his favourite filtered brand in his hand. 'Well, yes I do, actually.'

'No, I mean, have you got one for me?'

'Well, I don't think that's a very good idea …'

'If it isn't a good idea, perhaps I should take that one off your hands.'

'Touché.'

Kenneth cautiously hands Mac a cigarette, lights it for him with his silver lighter, initialled KM in elaborate script, steps back from Mac to take in some November air, turns to leave.

'I'm Mac,' coughs the older man, now clouded in blue smoke.

'Kenneth.'

Kenneth looks surprised that he has said this, starts to back-pedal towards the front of the town hall.

'What's the meeting about, mate?'

Kenneth hesitates.

'Ah …'

'You don't know?'

'Yes, *I* organized it,' his words whiplash.

'About us rough sleepers, is it?'

'About health care … for the homeless, yes.'

'What health care is *that* exactly?'

Kenneth butts his cigarette. He is starting to sweat. The sun has come out from behind the dark clouds. He wants to get to the sandwich in his case lying on the chair in the back row, where he watched over the morning's proceedings.

Mac continues, 'What time am I on, then?'

'What! I beg your pardon?'

'You brought an expert in from Germany and I'm sitting right here in front of you, aren't I? You don't actually want to know what this life is like, do you?'

'Doctor Fischer from Berlin has done a statistical analysis—'

Mac belches loudly. 'That's bullshit and you know it. It's Mercedes research.'

'I beg your pardon,' Kenneth shrugs.

'He drove by a homeless man in his Mercedes and made a note in his little black book.'

Mac smiles, stretches out in the sunshine.

Kenneth reddens and points a rigid finger toward Mac. 'Listen, I'm sorry to put it this way, but you are in no position to judge Doctor Fischer, his research or our conference. We are actually working very hard to make life better for ... I've got to go back in. Stay out of the doorway!'

'Pompous ass.'

*

There are clowns on the television, clowns and little children, dancing, holding hands, singing songs. 'Ring a ring of roses ...'

The door opens but Kenny doesn't look up from the show, his favourite. Every Thursday. The stepfather opens the refrigerator, drops several ice cubes into a glass and pours an amber liquid over them.

'What are you watching, Kenny?'

'Nothing.'

'Why don't we turn it off, then?'

'Cause I'm watching, sort of.'

'Smart ass.'

'Where's my mum?'

'She's working late tonight.'

'Again?'

'Yes, again.'

Kenny switches off the television. 'I'm going to my room now.'

The stepfather drains his glass. 'Why don't you come and sit with me a minute, Kenny?'

'You smell like whiskey again.'

'I've just had this one. It will be okay. Don't you worry. Come on over here. We haven't had a good talk in a quite a while, have we, son?'

'No, I'm going to my room.'

The stepfather flushes with anger. 'I told you to come over here—'

'You're not my dad . . .'

The stepfather grows quiet, whispers. 'We've talked about that, haven't we? Come over here. You can sit beside me, read your book . . . I'll watch the news . . . You can just keep me company . . .'

Kenny fights off the tears he knows are coming. 'Mum said I don't have to *do* anything.'

The stepfather responds sharply, angrily. 'I said get over here – now.'

'No.'

'I'll tell your mother you were bad—'

'I don't care anymore. I'm going to my room. If you come up, I'll scream and Mrs Hood will come upstairs.'

Kenny then runs upstairs, slamming his bedroom door behind him.

The stepfather stands up, makes another drink, promptly spills it, curses under his breath. 'I'll bloody teach you a lesson, I will.'

He mounts the stairs heavily, opens Kenny's bedroom door.

'No, no, no—'

Kenny's scream is quickly muffled.

*

Mac takes a final swig from his plastic bottle of cider, wipes his mouth with the arm of his filthy jacket, stops to feel the warm buzz of the alcohol go through his body; he takes another long pull. Fuck the experts. Mac remembers the first time he got drunk. He laughs out loud, so hard he tears up slightly. He was young then, working, with a family, before it all turned upside down.

Mac is feeling warm all over. He finishes the bottle, tosses it towards the doorway. Discuss that! He moves closer. It looks like they are finishing up inside.

Kenneth shakes hands with a broad-shouldered man with coiffed grey hair who is wearing a nicely cut brown suit. The older man turns to leave but Kenneth continues shaking his hand. The conference has gone well. Kenneth will celebrate with a quick cigarette before closing things down. He steps outside, breathes in the scent of damp leaves, cheap cider and piss, then frowns.

Mac wants to ask Kenneth how it went but the slick young man looks too surly.

They are silent for a long time. Kenneth drags on his cigarette. Mac opens another bottle of cider. They watch an ambulance squeal towards the hospital, lost in their separate thoughts. Kenneth butts his cigarette and goes inside.

*

Inside the tiny seaside cottage an old clock ticks away the long day. Outside, harsh waves crash against the rocky beach.

'Course you've gone and bloody lost the boat now. You can't hold on to anything, can you? Next it will be the cottage, and then me, for God's sake. Is that the plan, then?'

'Bloody hell, but you know the fishin's no good. You know that. There's too many boats and not enough fish. And we had to take out that loan on it after you had your fall and stopped working at the shop in the village. You know that. Your own brother lost his boat to the same bleeding bank six weeks ago. You know that, don't you? You know all of it.'

He drops his cup into its saucer but she doesn't stir.

'I know it, alright.'

'Then what are you on about, woman?'

'You know.'

'Why don't you just say, it then? Go on. Get it out.'

'He never lost his son. My brother never lost his only bloody son.'

'What are you sayin'?'

'He never lost his son in the bloody North Sea. Not like you did. Our baby boy.'

Then she's sobbing and only the sea is louder as she makes no effort to stop the flow that's been building for so long. The dam's burst.

'Oh, Jesus.'

He stands up but remains fixed to the old hardwood floor, unable to move.

'I told you not to take him. I told you he was too young, ten years old, he was. Jesus, Mac, how could you? How could you? In God's name, how could you? Our only son and you went and bloody lost him in the sea.'

She falls to the floor weeping, now silently. For a long minute only the sea can be heard.

'It's this again, is it?' he says.

'It never goes,' she whispers.

He slowly walks to the other side of the room and opens the door of the battered bureau, takes out a folder of papers, waving them toward her. His face is red with anger and wet with tears.

'How could you accuse me of that again? You know what happened. You were sitting in the back row at the bleedin' inquest five years ago. You heard what the coroner said. He spelled it out: It was an a-c-c-i-d-e-n-t – accident.'

He reads: '"The death of Marc McAllister was an accident and no blame can be attached to any party, agency or institution." It's right here in black and white. Read it for yourself.'

He throws the papers onto the table where his wife had been sitting.

'Don't you think I wish that boy was here right now with us for our tea? That boy was my life. He was the only thing that mattered to me.'

He pulls out his handkerchief and blows loudly.

'And now he's gone,' she says coldly. 'And now, he's gone.'

She gets up, grabs a plate off the counter and throws it against the wall, smashing it into many pieces that scatter across the floor. He walks out of the room, slamming the door.

She wails after him.

'Go on then, you bastard, back to the pub, back to your mother, back to the city. I don't care where you go. You've lost him. You've lost the boat. You've lost it all for us. And now you're lost to me.'

*

The sun is setting and Mac needs to move closer to the doorway of the hall to secure his place for the night, keep warm. He gathers up his stinking belongings and winces at the odour. Kenneth appears in the doorway again.

'Hey, Doc.'

Kenneth can't help himself. He laughs.

'I'm not a doctor. Listen, I think I heard enough from you earlier. Just let me enjoy my cigarette in peace, will you? It's been a long day, a good day, but a long day, and I still have twenty things to do. Please.'

'They're addictive, you know.'

'There's a news flash. I'll get Doctor Fischer back and he can adjust his research. Thank you very much. It's just what I need to hear right now.'

'So, when does it start?'

'What's that?'

'My new healthcare plan?'

'Oh.'

'So?'

'It's . . . complicated . . .'

'And you think people on the street like me are too stupid or too fried to understand, right, mate? It's possible we know more about life on the streets than your fucking expert.'

'No, that's not it at all. It will take time . . .'

Mac is warming up in more than one way. 'Look, I may be pissed. In fact, I *am* pissed and I'm livin' on the streets and have been for a long bloody time. So take some of that damn time now and bring me up to date. This is my fucking life . . .'

'Okay, okay . . .'

'So, what did you learn?

'Put simply?'

'How else would I understand it?'

'Put simply, it would be better if no one was sleeping on the street.'

'Now who's got a news flash?

'There are shelters to start with . . .'

'Shelters?'

'Yes, they are not the answer, of course, but—'

'No bleeding thank you. I have been there. A hundred men sleepin' on a church basement floor, crying, shittin' themselves, fightin', stealin' from each other, sleepwalkin'. Fuck . . .'

'I understand . . .'

'Not bloody likely.'

'You'd be surprised.'

Mac is surprised. He takes a swig of cider. A new bottle.

'What do you know about it?'

'Never mind . . .'

'Come on, for a moment there I thought you were a bleedin' human bein', about to tell me something about yourself. Have you been on the street?'

'Not exactly,' Kenneth whispers.

'Well, what, exactly?'

'Forget it.'

'I can't, mate, I'm livin' it every day. Can you forget it?

'I already have.'

'Sure you have, mate. Sure you have.'

'Looks can be deceiving.'

'What the hell is that supposed to mean?'

'Some of us have been through all kinds of shit and pulled ourselves up. Some of us have found the personal discipline . . .'

Kenneth moves toward the doorway, wonders about lighting up another cigarette but puts the packet back in his pocket.

'Turned you hard, though, dinnit?'

'If you say so.'

'Bloody right, it did.'

'Fair enough . . .'

'What kind of place were you in?'

'Not important . . .'

'A hard one, aren't you?

'If you say so.'

Mac takes a long swig from his bottle of cider, belches but tries to disguise it, speaks quietly, looking Kenneth in the eye, 'What was it you were in, then?'

Kenneth's response is almost inaudible. 'Orphanage, group homes, juvie . . .'

'Did they hurt you?'

Kenneth moves toward Mac, raising his fist. Mac grimaces.

'I think you should just mind your own bloody business. I'll thank you to leave me in peace for a few moments before I close things down inside.' He opens the door to the town hall and spits out his final sentence, 'It's been a long bloody day, and you're frankly making it longer.'

'Course, don't go getting intimate with the homeless, it could complicate things. You might learn somethin', mess up your research. Best keep your distance. What's it the social worker told me back in the day? Oh, yeah. He had to stay *detached* if I'm sayin' it right. Or was it semi-detached? I can't remember. Truth was, he was a priss. I only asked him if he had kids himself. Fuck.'

Kenneth closes the door but stays outside, lights a cigarette, lets out a long sigh as he exhales. 'Okay, if we're being intimate, then tell me how you ended up here, living on the street, drinking that poison, smelling up the entrance to the bloody town hall, for Christ's sake.'

'Like you said, it's complicated.'

'Try me. I have a Masters in complicated.'

'Smart ass.'

'Touché.'

'I lost someone.'

'Jesus.'

Kenneth slowly approaches Mac.

'What are you doing?'

'Who was it?'

'Never bloody mind. And back the fuck off.'

'Now who's hard?'

There is a long pause. Mac takes another swig of the alcohol. Kenneth inhales his cigarette.

'Still can't talk about it. I can only drink about it. Anyways, it's none of your fucking business, is it?'

'You started it, mate. Now I see you're even more fucked up than I thought,' Kenneth adds bitterly.

'Kiss my arse.'

Mac tosses his cider bottle at the door as Kenneth retreats behind it, then pokes his head around one last time.

'I've had enough. I'm calling the police. You better move on right now. When I think of all our work to try and make things better . . . Move on.'

*

The stepfather slowly descends the stair, puts on the television news. Kenny's sobbing gets louder and louder.

'Mum, Mum, where are you? Mum ... Mrs Hood, why didn't you call the police? Somebody, please help me. He bloody did it again.'

*

A police car, siren blaring, screeches around a corner and stops. Two doors open and slam shut again almost in unison.

A passer-by calls out, 'You're too late, mates. He's gone.'

The police radio crackles.

'Are you sure?'

'Yes.'

'Where'd he go?'

'Couldn't tell you.'

'You're sure he's not here?'

'Definitely moved on.'

'If you see him again, give us a call, will you?'

'Course I will.'

They climb back in the police car and it disappears down the road, siren wailing, lights flashing. Then all that can be heard is the sound of two trains clicking by one another on the nearby railway tracks.

A Life of Bliss

I can hear everything that's happening next door. They don't build walls this flimsy any more, but the squat old hotel overlooking that triumphal church spire on the heath is not up to today's building codes. The couple next door had a brawl last night. He tried to punch her and missed. I swear I could see his fist bulging through the wall as he cursed at the top of his voice.

'Fucking hell.'

Then she shrieked back at him. 'You bastard. How dare you!'

It didn't start out that way. Earlier soft Diana Krall jazz had wafted through the paper-thin wall, mood music for the distinct rhythms of slow lovemaking that started soon after they checked in at lunch time.

'That's so good, do that again,' she whispered hoarsely, sounding as if she had spent the morning at Cheltenham cheering her favourite horse, her moaning matching the banging of the headboard against the wall, faster, faster, a great sigh, and then nothing. I honestly didn't try to listen in. It was very loud. They say you can hear clearly if you place a glass on the wall and hold your ear up to it, but I didn't do that.

This morning I can't hear anything. He went out an hour ago, closing the door quietly behind him, as if not to disturb her sleeping. A few moments later an overweight balding man in his forties wearing a black raincoat left the hotel, turning right towards the grubby pub a few doors down. But I can't be sure if that was him or not. He could still be in the restaurant tearing into the full English. The aroma of overcooked bacon and strong coffee turns my stomach. There's not a sound from next door now, no silky jazz, no gentle snoring, no election blather from men in blue suits blaring from the television, not even the soft spray of shower water on the ancient bathroom tiles.

I think he may have killed her.

My room is simple, barely large enough to hold the queen-sized bed with deep purple bedspread and big fat pillows. There's a small television and I watch on mute to see which way the man in the middle at Westminster is leaning, while keeping an ear out. It was once a good hotel and still bills itself as the finest Georgian establishment in this part of the city. But I don't think I am in the best part of the old block. The room looks nothing like the one I saw pictured on the internet, all white walls and pale ash furniture with sunlight flooding through the old-fashioned wide windows that practically run the height of the room. Mine is darker, gloomy with perhaps the original eighteenth-century furnishings, brown wood with deep recesses from bottles, glasses and cigarettes, vestiges of past affairs. But for the time being it is home. It is comfortable enough and no one disturbs me.

I need this time away. It is better for everyone. The family home, a tiny flat in a jigsaw development flatteringly called Heather Gardens, is only a few blocks away. Meg should be finishing her breakfast of coffee and plain brown toast before heading off to catch the train to work. But these are not normal times. Otherwise I wouldn't be here. There's a helicopter overhead just now, whirly birds, we used to call them when we were kids, and I can still see and hear why, long blades whirling above, puncturing the quiet morning on the heath. I wonder if they are watching the room next door.

I grab a quick lunch at the pub, more for the pints of lager than the bloody half-cooked burger, so dripping with grease I leave most of it on the plate. It's a busy establishment with lots of youngsters about and the staff members are so harassed they rarely have time to clean the wobbly old tables. The bloke behind the bar with the spiked blond hair says the election was a waste of time. He's waiting for the real competition of the summer, the World Cup.

'England has a chance, if the Italian gaffer plays it right,' he chirps like he almost believes himself over the din. I don't linger. I want to get back to my room. It isn't the post-election drama – the lesser blue suit is now being wooed by the left, the telly says – I want to find out what is going on with my neighbours in the next room. There's more music now, folk or country, maybe the poetic wailings of Lucinda Williams, but it's too low to be sure.

Then I hear the man speaking in a monotone. He is reading, a document with lots of legal words, I think. Is it a will? It's definitely his voice but there is no response from her. I listen into the night. There is no music now, only soft rhythmic snoring. I think it is him. Every once in a while I hear someone crying into a pillow.

In the morning I try phoning home. After a dozen rings, I hang up. Meg should be there. It's her day off from the care home. She does the books for the administrator. She knows where the waste is. It's what they kept talking about during the General Election. But the home is private, not National Health Service. I guess they have waste too. I'll try and phone again later, sort things out. It will be fine. Things have always worked themselves out.

We met at school. She was pretty, short, with tossed brown hair, inquiring eyes, a straightforward manner. She liked me, she said. I was gobsmacked. What, me? We went to lunch at the tea pavilion in Greenwich Park. We sat at the round picnic tables outside in the pissing rain, huddling together under our hoods. She kissed me on the lips, her mouth tasting faintly of carrot muffin. I was hooked.

That was a long time ago, a very long time ago. I don't know how these things happen. One minute you're living off love's adrenalin, can't get enough of each other, feasting on body and soul, the next you're staring across the divide and there's a wall of blue lurching like border control between the two of you. Of course, there's a lot of life between the one minute and the next. That's all I'm going to say.

I hear yet another high-pitched squeal of a siren and check out my window. It's a police car headed towards Woolwich. But mostly it's been quiet outside. It's raining and there is none of the usual jet traffic arcing towards the airport because of that volcanic ash from Iceland. Is it revenge? That's what somebody on the television wonders. I still have the sound down but the subtitles spit out the words of the smiling blonde presenter a few seconds behind the images. Not only did the Greens win a seat in Parliament but the airports are shut. Everything's changing. It's confusing. There's no word yet on a deal among the suits but the bald reporter with funny glasses says the man in the middle is now leaning right.

I think they're burning incense next door. I half expect to hear eastern chanting, but there's nothing, only silence. Then the door closes, softly. The heavyset man leaves the hotel, this time turning left towards the village. He's carrying his long black raincoat and is limping slightly. He's in no hurry. I still smell the faint exotic scent, which reminds me of serving Mass when we were children up north, or that Indian shop in the city where I bought Meg that expensive wicker table two years ago. She loved it.

It wasn't the affair that started the spiral downwards, more the slow drift the few years before, too much time spent chasing sales, the almighty pound, and the sweet secretaries. I'm an estate agent in the city, or I was until a few months ago. The business tanked for a bit and I was vulnerable because I made a few mistakes, missed appointments, that sort of thing, nothing serious, really. Then it was the drinking and the snorting. I've stopped all that now, well the snorting anyway. Meg said it made me angry. I couldn't tell you what I was feeling. Perhaps I was out of control. She says I hit her a few times when I was high or drunk or both but I don't remember anything of it. The truth is I'd never hurt her. I've never been that way, not like my dad. Of course, it was hard when she was the only one earning a salary.

The kids are gone now. The lad's in Canada making a mint with a Toronto bank, and his sister's back and forth between Australia and New Zealand, trying to make up her mind which country has the best-looking lads. Meg's money is on the Kiwis. But we still have a mortgage and the new silver Mini in the driveway. We're not over the hump yet.

I'm working my way through an Indian takeaway of bland lamb korma and white rice when I hear them again. The television is turned down. The politicians are talking about expanding the Westminster vocabulary with a new word: coalition. I think it means they have to work together, cooperate. God forbid. But next door there is a strange kind of hubbub. I move closer to the wall without even noticing. Several voices speak at once, like a badly run meeting, or that television show where the politicians always talk over each other. It's not the television. It's almost as if someone is holding court, weighing evidence from one side then the next. Then they all speak at once again. I make out some words: 'custody', 'beneficiary', 'property'.

Then it's quiet and I hear the television blasting sound for the pictures on my set, two men in matching smiles meeting at Number 10 Downing Street, patting each other on the back, well done. The door opens and closes quietly. I look outside but no one exits the hotel. Again, I hear crying and I think he speaks harshly to her.

'You asked for this, darling, didn't you?' Did she?

Meg left me soon after the kids moved out. She wanted to find herself, said she'd be back. I was at sea. I'd get up and go to work every day. The economy was good then and I was busy enough, selling flats all over Greenwich and Lewisham, tiny ones, four bedrooms with winding staircases, everything was going fast and inflated. But my heart wasn't in it. Meg would phone some nights. I used to rush home after work to be there for her call, then head to the pub and drown my sorrows in Speckled Hen, chased with Jameson's. She went to California to visit her sister but that didn't last because she didn't have enough money to keep up with the daily trips to the great sprawling Oakland malls or the Friday-night country club dinners, triple martinis and enough red meat to put you on the slab in the morgue.

She came home after three months. I think she ran out of money, but she said she missed me, and so we tried to pick up where we had left off. The kids had gone and now we had to find things to talk about across the table of fish and chips and mushy peas. Meg began bringing books to the supper, some South American named Paulo Coelho, and Dan Brown, the guy who writes about demons and stuff. I drifted to the telly, or the pub.

They're making love next door again. The music is louder, Amy Winehouse's 'You Know I'm No Good', and they are quieter, less frantic. Their breathing is one. Meanwhile on the television two very handsome men in their forties – I can no longer tell them apart – are walking through a garden looking like they are about to embark on a life of bliss. Bless them. This coalition thing looks kind of like gay marriage, but what do I know? I try Meg again but there is still no answer. The sun is peeking through the clouds over the heath. The church spire seems smaller somehow, less majestic. Jets have started to fly again. Perhaps Iceland has had its moment. I think about going for a walk through the village, checking out the dishevelled used book store across from the church to see if they have something for Meg. I'm sure we can make it right, if she would only answer the phone. I can't go to the house, not just yet. I lie down and try to sleep. I drift in and out of that dream where I am being tied up, smothered. I thought I was finished with that but it's back again. Then I hear jets, screaming sirens, whirly birds. I pull the pillow over my head.

I wake up to the sound of laughter in the room next door. I have no idea what time it is. My head aches and I notice the empty whiskey bottle on the ancient desk. I hear the snapping and zipping of suitcases, laughter that says, 'Fooled you!'

Then there is a loud knock.

'It's the police.' The voice is deep, serious. He's not going to get away with it, after all. I'm not sure whether to laugh or cry.

The knock is louder next time! Bang, bang, bang. It can't be my door, can it? I open the door and see that tall policeman Meg called before. I suddenly remember the purple under her eye. He wants to talk to me. I point toward the couple from next door, retreating down the corridor, arm-in-arm, oblivious to the policeman. I open my mouth but only my breath escapes. Then they are gone. The policeman fixes his steel-grey eyes on me.

'Sir, we need to talk. Do you remember meeting me before?'

I shrug.

'Sir, you need to come with me to the station. This morning neighbours in the flat next door to yours found your wife suffocated in her bed. Do you have anything to say at this time?'

I want to tell him about the people in the next room, the lovemaking, the fighting, the music, and the tricks. His eyes are piercing. He will not understand. I shrug again, say nothing.

*

My cell is tiny with a single bed, a sink, toilet and a mirror. I avoid the mirror. There's a strong stench of piss. I think I have been here a week. I have a lawyer coming in a few minutes. I'm sure he can clear this up. It's just a misunderstanding. I've never hurt anybody in my life. I want to phone Meg but they tell me I can't. There's no telly here so I don't know how the coalition is working out. How long will it last? Maybe the man in the next cell knows something. He just arrived today. He already has a visitor. I move closer to his side of the cell so I can hear. But I think they are plotting something. They sound like they are from some other place, or they are speaking in code. So I move closer to the wall. Maybe I can get some information, help the authorities out. They are whispering but I can hear everything they are saying.

Going Home

Rose

Come faster, my lorry, my lover, split me in two, like so many tried before, soft men and hard men, sweet young lovers and rapists, like the policeman, who used his baton to colour my cheek and change my face forever, and that man I used to call husband, I now call bastard. This is why I hide behind my rough wool scarves and that umbrella I found outside the train station, where I used to sleep on that bench on quiet afternoons until that all-about-Jesus man selling magazines told the police I was bothering him and they pushed my rusting shopping cart up the ramp, telling me to go somewhere I belong. But I don't fit in anywhere. I hear what they mutter when they pass by that sunny bench in the rose garden, where I sleep some nights – like fat Arab bitch or stinking cunt. Do they think I don't know I smell? I have not had a hot bath since that bastard ran away with his boss's wife, taking the money that was going to get me a train ticket so I could visit my daughter. The landlord threw me out. I am not Arab. They should know that but they don't care because they think that all people who stink or who they hate are Arab. I am also not as fat as they think, either. I cover myself in layers of clothes that I find. This is my body. I no longer offer it to anyone. Except you, my lover, my lorry, come to me now, split me open. Divide the good and the bad. Send the bad part of me – that left her daughter with strangers far away – to hell; and bring the good part of me – that is so sorry for stabbing that boy near the tea hut – to heaven. I am tired and I pray this lorry will help me go see God or the devil – I don't really care – so come, lorry, come, my lover, my final lover. Come …

Lorry Driver

Last run before Christmas. Thank God. Not that I believe in all that – God or Christmas. Christmas goes with family. That's long gone. It's just me now in my room down in Woolwich. The loo's down the hall. I share it with that black landlady. Not that I ever see her. Sometimes Sherry from the café comes for a cuppa and a roll around on my creaking bed. She's too skinny for me but she'll stay longer if I ask her nice. I'm usually okay since I quit drinking. God, what's that? It can't be. At this hour? Get off the fucking road. Sherry says I'm okay sober, almost sweet. But she won't stay the whole night. Not with my landlady watching, listening to the old bed. Move, lady, get rid of the cart. God, all I wanted was a few days off, lying about with Sherry. Move, lady, O God …

Acknowledgements

The Memory Girl was previously published in *Litro* magazine. *Playing Catch* appeared in *The Toronto Star.*

I would like to thank my first readers for their encouragement and critique. Some would rather remain anonymous, I'm sure, but I will single out Claire Asling, Martin Asling, Sara Beth Grasby, Cathy Higaki, William MacKinnon, Dean Salter, Jeffrey Warren, Amanda Harper, Rae Struthers, Michael Sargent, the Blackheath Creative Writers, Sue Browning, and most of all, Patricia Hughes. Any mishaps remain mine alone.

The cover photo is courtesy of Richard C. Choe. 'The Broken Man' is a life-size sculpture by artist Willard Spence, which is on permanent display at Ghost Ranch in Abiquiu, New Mexico.